Saved By The
ORC

RENA MARKS

SAVED
<u>BY THE ORC</u>

He saved me, even when his kind destroyed my family.

Joanna: When orcs invaded our village, everything changed. The newly self-appointed mayor chose me as his wife—no matter what my choice had been. Living taxes were imposed—if you want to live, you pay.

My new husband pays the tax for both of us, and it keeps me working wage-free in his eatery for my room and board.

But then comes the day when everyone else in our town hides because the orcs return for us.

---

*L*atsil: My scars aren't the honorable sort among our people. Mine were forged by capture when my mate sold me to another clan.

I returned home upon her death, broken hearted and in denial that she was one who'd betrayed me. But part of me knows the truth and for that reason, I'll never re-mate. A decision that's challenged when I save a beautiful female from the clan who once imprisoned me. A female who's left her human husband and—like me—is determined never to mate again.

*Trigger warnings: This book contains situations, sexual and otherwise, as well as violence and/or abuse, both real and implied, that may be disturbing for some readers. If you are offended by these subjects, please do not buy this book.

Prologue

Quick Note: If you enjoy Saved By The Orc, be sure to check out the next one in the series, **Bought By The Orc**! With that, enjoy!

*J**oanna, wife to the Mayor of Granby:***

"Your village is an utter ghost town."

The leader of the orcs who rode into town with his guard is the only one of them unscarred by battle. His voice is surprisingly pleasant, well-modulated, as if he's been speaking English his entire life. I try hard not to stare at the tusks that jut from his lip but because he speaks the language without any accent, I'm intrigued instead of flat-out terrified.

"Welcome to Granby." My voice is wry, and he grins as if he understands sarcasm.

Does he? Again, my curiosity peaks.

'Tis true, the entire village, smaller than most, has headed indoors to hide. Including my self-appointed husband, the Mayor of Granby. When my parents died in the last orc attack—in which the brutal Blackheart clan of monsters destroyed half the town and then, to everyone's surprise, up and left—Homer McLinn made himself leader. He then announced he'd need a wife and grabbed my arm.

No ceremony. No permission. No blessing from the Lord. Nothing but his decision.

Homer McLinn also decided to force me to leave the eatery open for business while everyone else—himself included—remained in hiding. He'd determined a pretty face might satisfy these new orcs until our males returned from the range.

Pussy.

And while I should be terrified out of my mind because orcs slaughtered half our town, I'm just kind of numb. My life has been a living hell since losing my parents in the previous attack and quite frankly, I no longer care if I'm slaughtered.

But these strange orcs don't look like they're about to attack. They don't dress like the Blackhearts, who are known for wearing black leather in the heat of summer. They just wear less—loincloths instead of britches, vests instead of tunics. They can be seen from a distance because the black is decoratively stitched with gold thread.

"You ever travel to the neighboring town? Serenity?" The unscarred one asks.

Serenity. My sister city. Or so I had thought as a child. The leader of that land, Lord Montierge, had galloped through our town with a carriage behind his horse. He'd blasted in long enough to ask if we'd known of another town nearby large enough for a hospital. His little girl was sick, and he'd do anything to cool the raging fevers that plagued her.

I'd often wondered what it would be like to have my father so dedicated. Not that he was a bad father—he did turn down Homer McLinn when he asked for my hand—but I couldn't imagine him leaving his farm long enough to care about whether I lived or died.

I'd fantasized about that little girl often. She was a true lady, titled through her father. I even knew her name. Lady Hannah Montierge of Serenity. Throughout my formative years I'd pretend that we'd been friends, best friends, closer than sisters. I'd spend summers in her town, and she'd spend winters in mine. I'd teach her how to grow vegetables, and she'd teach me fine manners. How to serve tea.

Now the idea almost makes me snort aloud. I serve all right, though it's not with fine bone China teacups. It's massive metal plates, fit for the brave males we have left.

He still waits for my response.

"No. I mean, as a child, probably. Not recently, though."

"Hmm. So, you don't know any of the townspeople?"

"None at all."

Because I'd like for these interesting ones to stay—I mean, why not, it breaks up the monotony of my life—I gesture to a table. I find it curious that these orcs are so different than the last sort, and I'd like to know why. Besides, if they'd wanted to, they'd already have carted me off.

"You'd serve us?" Grunts the largest orc to the right of the leader. Gah, he's the most terrifying out of all of them. His eyes are lined with kohl, maybe it's tattooed, his ear has been mangled and has healed rather badly. Lighter green slashes adorn the darker green skin of his body in strategic spots. Scars, I realize. He's been cut and marred—even his lip has a whitish-green line bisected through it. But his muscles are massive, and the scars decorate instead of detract.

I shrug and the humor of the situation hits me. My "husband" cowers upstairs in a closet, the townspeople are sealed up tight in the hidden rooms of their homes, praying the orcs don't light fire to the second half of the town—despite the fact that Mayor McLinn pays them their newly imposed living tax—and I can make them, all the *brave* townsfolk, suffer a wee bit more in the hidden safety of their panic rooms. In the heat. It's the least I can do considering all of them were willing to sacrifice me instead.

With a dark twinkle in my eye, I nod to the huge, massively scarred one. "You've been riding, yes? You stopped by for a reason. Have a meal and I'll make all my other hungry customers wait." I wave my arm at the empty tables as if others truly sit and scowl while I take my time with the strangers.

Several orcs look around at the other tables as if I'm addled in the head.

I leave them while I pop into the kitchen area to serve up the specials. I've gotten used to running Homer's. Used to be, Homer was the one who ran the kitchen but since I "married" him, he needs to focus on his mayoral duties, so I earn my keep by running his business.

Not that anyone knows what mayoral duties entail. It's a new-fangled term he'd heard somewhere and decided to appoint himself as such.

I startle when a large green hand stretches for the stack of bowls I'm struggling to reach in a cabinet built for larger men. One of them followed me into the kitchen. He easily brings the entire spare stack down to the counter for me to reach.

For a brief moment, true fear makes my heart pound. My palms tingle with the adrenaline rush from being this close to one. Obviously, he was sent to make sure I don't poison the troops and well, I can't say I blame him. But it's disorienting to have someone so huge breathe down your slender neck.

"Thank you," I murmur, taking the top bowl from the stack and ladling the chili into it.

I stack the bowl onto the tray and reach for the next one, filling it quickly and adding the bowl to the tray. When all the bowls are filled, I add the soup spoons and head to the cold storage for some fresh bread and cheese to complete the meal.

And then I heft the tray up with nary a grunt—I've been cuffed enough over the last months to work without complaint—and carry it to the table where the orcs sit. Quickly I dole out the meals, then serve the drinks—my own concoction of sweet peach juice and tea. The hovering orc still stands by my side, watching as if making sure the drinks aren't tainted.

I guess I can't blame him.

The leader doesn't eat, even though I've served him.

I take a bowl for myself, blowing on the spoonful before jamming it into my mouth. "See?" I say, fanning the burn on my tongue. "'Tis safe. I'm not about to take on a half dozen males twice my size. Eat up."

"Why are you serving us?" The leader asks, taking his bowl and tentatively tasting.

I shrug. "Breaks up the monotony of my day, I guess."

"I see you don't have many people to talk to," the leader says shrewdly.

I smile, reaching for a chunk of fresh baked bread, and then can't help but snicker. He knows the village folk are hiding, but what really makes me chuckle is that I'm eating well without a husband about to slap my hands and remind me the food is for the customers. Instead, here I sit, at a table full of orcs, eating my fill like a queen. Why, it was just last week that I stole a chunk of bread and pocketed it into my apron but was so exhausted from the day's labor I forgot to eat it. I found it during the next day's laundry, a sogged mess to scoop out.

Before long, I realize I'm the first to finish. No matter. I calmly get up and serve myself another portion, then bring my bowl back and sit as if nothing is wrong.

The scarred orc—the beastly one—sits across from me and grins as if pleased by my appetite. It looks awkward and unpracticed, and the others look confused as their gazes bounce from me to him, but then they all decide to toss aside what little manners they'd been practicing and start shoveling the food into their mouths.

Several get up on their own for seconds and I don't mind one whit. Nothing like eating with the customers, even the non-paying kind who hopefully won't kill you when they leave. If they do, though, at least I'll go with a full belly.

When everything is all said and done, they stand and stretch, some walking around, and I'm sure Homer listens with an ear to the wall, probably hoping for my screams. Instead, the scarred one—who looks rather interesting, like he has a story to tell with so many more scars than the rest—tosses me a pouch that jingles.

"For your service," he says, and the other orcs look at each other.

Maybe they'd meant to kill me, then? My heart stutters because surely this means they've changed their minds?

"Thank you, milord," I whisper, suddenly aware of any carrying sounds. "Be safe on your journeys."

He grunts and one by one, they leave the eatery—and me—behind. And as I watch the horses prance about as they mount, a sudden idea comes to me.

He gave me coin. Unsure of how much, but orcs deal mostly in gold. Not that I expect that, of course. Their meal was only worth a copper each, but he gave me a bag full. Why try hiding it from Homer, who will search me when he sees all the empty dishes? I can keep the whole bag, even if it's a handful of coppers, it'll buy me enough meals, maybe a room for the night while I get a job somewhere in Serenity.

'Twould be nice if I could get a sewing job in a seamstress shop. All women because I've had my fill of men.

Why not pretend the orcs dragged me away? Why not hop on a faithful old mare—everyone is in hiding and not minding the stables—and make my way to Serenity, where I can start anew? A name. A made-up background. I can even meet my childhood friend, for real this time.

As they gallop away, I suck in a deep breath, and—before I can change my mind—emit an ear-piercing scream. "No! Take your hands off me! Why did you stay behind? No, stop! Don't stuff that horrid thing in my mouth—"

I stop abruptly, pretend I'm choking, and then toss a few heavy pans about to crash into the walls. It feels really good to throw the heavy dishes around—the chili staining the whitewashed walls with red paste—knowing that someone else will have to clean this mess.

And then I toss a couple of the pots into the windows, the crashing of the glass sounding somewhat musical to my ears. Not a curtain outside flutters, the townspeople keeping to their word of not emerging from their hiding spots until the church bells ring.

Someone was expected to ring them and that someone will not be me. No, it'll be up to Mayor McLinn to ring his own goddamn bells once the bastard is done pissing his pants in the hidden panel of the wall.

I grab the last loaf of bread and cheese, wrapping it into a towel and shoving it into a light pot that I may need for cooking, grab Homer's spare flint from the pantry closet and, just as I'm about to close the door, notice a spare canteen hooked with others on the wall. Greedy man doesn't even know how much crap he has. Just demands things from out of towners if they can't afford his outrageous prices. I don't even take the time to fill it. Nope, I'm out of here, and I'll gather water from a stream once I'm safely away.

Quietly now, I slide from the door and tiptoe along the wooden porch, then slip between buildings to get to the stable. Once inside, the noise from the animals actually startles me; I'm so used to the dead silence of the rest of the village. I shush the nervous horses and then narrow my eyes at the most majestic steed of the lot. Pegasus.

My husband's prized possession.

No sense stealing an aging brood mare, right? No orc would take a stumbling miss. No, the orc would steal the finest beast of the stable.

I whistle softly. "Pegasus, come. There you go, have an apple." I grab the entire bag of them from the hook on the door and saddle him up. I'm nervous, which makes him nervous, because this feels like it's taking forever and a day. But there's still nary a peep from the silent town and I force myself to take a deep breath to calm.

And finally, I'm ass-to-saddle onto Pegasus and have him calmly *walk* right out of town.

Chapter One

*J*oanna:

As soon as we hit the trail, we fly. Air whips through my hair as we charge through the dust.

I can't believe I got away. My heart had pounded so hard, I was sure it might explode in my chest. Even now, I'm sure I may have nightmares about Homer chasing me. I've feared him so, even before my parents' death, and I was sure he was going to ask my father for my hand. But right now, I'm free and I chase the debilitating fear away.

Best bet, though the road leads straight to Serenity, is to get off the trail and into the wooded area. Not right away, of course, it's at least a day's ride to the neighboring town. Nay, I'll ride until Pegasus is tired and I am sore, then when the sun is no longer hot, we'll explore the forest for a creek, or a small rock ledge to hide beneath. I'll feed the horse, mayhap snack on one of his apples myself, though I have the bread and cheese still. As soon as daylight breaks, we'll make good time to get to Serenity.

I'm somewhat wary of running into the orcs again. I'd just left a few minutes after them so there's a good possibility I will. It's safest to stay hidden for the night. They may have let me go once, but it isn't guaranteed they'll do it again. Though, they seemed quite different from the orcs known as Blackheart. I'm not sure if I caught their clan name, but I guess it doesn't matter none. Hopefully, I'll never see green brutes again.

Eventually Pegasus slows, and I'm okay with that. He takes to trotting and so I steer him into the huge, wooded area that neighbors us with Serenity. We're nowhere near yet, but at least being off the trail keeps us a little safer.

When the sun's not so hot, I lead him to a creek. I'm able to fill my canteen and let Pegasus munch a bit. All at once I realize how unprepared I am for sleeping in the woods. All I have are the clothes on my back, though I guess my apron can double as a blanket. Well, sheet is more like it. But it's okay. It's worth it to be free.

Quickly I pull out the coin purse from deep within my cleavage and shake it into my hand.

And nearly faint at the sight.

I stare at the coins, thinking mayhap my eyes deceive me. They don't look like coppers. They don't look anything like silver.

It is gold, and not one coin per plate. It is a handful—an orc-sized hand—of gold.

Sweat breaks out at the nape of my neck. This will indeed buy me a room for the night, for many nights as I hunt for a job. Unless...

The orc had a pouch for each type of coin. He may have decided to be generous and give me the entire purse but gave me the gold instead of the copper.

Horror curdles the happiness I'd just felt by staring at the coin. The orc—the big, brutish scarred beast—will be back for his gold. Of that, I have no doubt. Quickly, I dump the gold back into the purse and bury it back into my bosom.

Numbly, I settle down with Pegasus, feeding him an apple and letting him graze the grass while I eat my bread and cheese. I splurge on one of the apples and then feed him another when I hear noises. Alarm prickles, tingling down my arms, the hair standing on end. At first, I think I am paranoid, still thinking about my dilemma with the coin. But then Pegasus whinnies, and I know something is amiss. Quietly, I pat him, trying to silently hush him. I need to saddle him in case we need to race far and fast. Before I get the chance, three orcs emerge from the trees.

They're not the same orcs from earlier, that much is clear. They look brutally savage in a different way, wearing loincloths that barely cover their beefy thighs. They love their black leather; one has a bag flung across his chest, the intricate gold lacing standing out. Another wears a black leather armband with the same gold stitch. Each orc easily spans two of me, and I wonder how fast I can run. Next to me, Pegasus whinnies.

"What have we here?" One moves right up to me. I move to jump onto the horse bareback but two move in, one grabbing me and the other grabbing Pegasus. They form a triangle. Pegasus rears in alarm.

"Fine animal," the one to my left says.

"Fine female," the other who grips me says and his tone leaves nothing to the imagination. I'm his to do with as he wants and he's letting us all know he claims me.

"She's mine." The first one growls, surprising me.

And the two fire off in rapid Orcish. The one holding me pulls his belt and quickly ties my hands together and then ties me to a tree. The third orc seems more concerned with Pegasus than anything else.

Like animals, the thundering orcs circle each other, feigning as if intending to make the other flinch, until it gets to be too much, and violence explodes. The sheer brutality keeps me watching spellbound as they throw each other into trees. When the one who'd tied my hands fails to get up, I think it's over.

But the other picks up a boulder and smashes his head—and then it's over. The one bleeding on the ground waves his hand weakly, and the winner turns to me.

He shifts his junk and the orc holding Pegasus grunts. The orc laid out on the ground groans. Then he slowly gets up and starts to build a fire as if nothing is wrong. They keep up a steady stream of Orcish, which I can't understand, but then two of them leave.

I'm left alone with the groaning orc who still rolls around on the dirty ground. If ever there was a chance to get away, this would be it. Quickly I pull at the ties at my wrists, but they hold strong. At least my hands are tied in front. I'm so busy messing with the ties I hardly notice when the two orcs come stomping back, with three small rabbits between them.

The leader—or at least, the one who won me—unties me from the tree, not even caring that he's getting blood all over my dress. He leaves my hands tied while he slices meat off the animals and then pushes it to me.

"Cook." His voice is a growl and... oh, God, when did I get used to being bossed like that? I find myself responding, jerking in place, and then hunting around their sloppy camp for a pot or pan. He laughs while I clumsily drag it to the fire and carefully place it without burning myself.

The second orc tosses a few potatoes at me and a lone carrot, but at least it's large. I grab the meat, throwing it into the hot pan while it sizzles.

The orc dangles a knife in front of me, his eyes narrowed as if he dares me to take it. I'll chop his potatoes, his carrots. And while I saw the strength and skill they fight with, it proves that I don't have the strength to take three of them on tonight, but one day, I'll gut him while he sleeps.

I left my forced husband. I'll leave the one who imprisons me too. It may not be with me untouched, but I lost my virginity a long time ago.

A lone voice calls out from behind the trees and the three in the camp draw their blades. But, like a giant wall stretching around the small camp, a line of six scarred orcs and their unscarred leader step in.

The ones from earlier.

The same group I was afraid would seek me out for their gold. I would gladly turn back time and race Pegasus after them to return the coin purse now that I know what the alternative turned out to be.

None of them act as if they know me in the slightest and why should they? They probably don't want to call attention to how much of their gold I'm holding onto.

The leader of the larger group speaks out in Orcish, and he seems calm when the orc who's claimed me shakes his head, refusing to do whatever he's asked. But then it's obvious that the new group is pretending to be friendly—or else it's obvious to my captors that they're outnumbered more than two to one. So huge, tusky-toothed grins break out as the orcs become wary forced friends. Fake friends, as my captor gestures for the new ones to sit on a tree stump near my cooking fire.

And my captor grabs me by the arm and pushes me toward the canteen cups to ladle out the steaming rabbit stew. He seems to take great joy in barking at me, then letting loose great bales of laughter when I flinch.

My hands are so closely tied together that it's like working one handed, since I have to grip everything with both hands, set it down, grab the ladle, scoop some stew, ladle it in, set down the ladle, pick up the cup and hand it to an orc.

The pretty orc takes it and to my surprise, the scarred one who always sits next to him grabs my wrist. He swiftly unknots a couple of pieces to remove the rope, barking something at the orc who claims me, who shrugs as if it's no big deal.

More surprising is when he notices a burn and a couple of nicks with the blade I used and rubs my knuckle gently.

He turns and I head back to the stew, ladling it out much more quickly without my bindings. I'm able to make it stretch so there's at least a half a cup for all the males and nothing for me, but it's okay. I'm still full from my own meager meal and the bountiful chili I'd feasted on earlier in the day.

So, I sit, holding as still as possible, while they make small talk I can't understand.

I think I see the scarred one—the right-hand man to the pretty leader—look my way, but his look is blank by the time I swerve my gaze to him.

When the meal is done, there's more gesturing from my owner, indicating the newcomers are welcome to spread out near the fire.

The orc who'd taken a beating earlier shoves some bedrolls to my new owner, who spreads his out away from the others and then points at me to come.

He stands waiting, rubbing his swollen cock. He intends to take me in front of everyone. I'm not as brave as I thought because there's no way I can do this, not without a battle. I get up to run, but he catches me quickly and grips my hair, then begins dragging me across the dirt.

Chapter Two

L *atsil, first guard to Brun, the West Mountain Orcs:*
      My blood boils when he drags her off to his bedroll by the hair. He intends to force her with all of us listening, with his own males watching. Mayhap he'll even share the girl with them. Even though I've fought hard to reestablish my reputation, I can't help but stand and utter the challenge to fight.

The orc freezes, his eyes narrowed on me. Next to me, Brun also stills. I know what he's thinking, I didn't have to challenge. We outnumber them more than two to one and can easily overtake them. But I want the female clear and free and that means I have to kill him so his friends can return to the clan and repeat that it was a fair challenge, or the Blackhearts will always hunt her down as their property.

It also gives him the upper hand as he is allowed to determine my crutch. Will he make me fight blindfolded? My hands tied? Bound to a tree? I wouldn't put any of it past him.

The female is lucky it was a quick meeting in Serenity, the town just north of hers. We'd stopped to scope the area around it, finding her town there, and then she served us, and we ate. When we left, we headed to Serenity, half of us hiding in the woods while some went into the city to sign a marriage contract between Prince Brun and the Lady Hannah. It was in the foul woods that we noticed an orc's steed running for his freedom—and then my own horse was startled by a rattlesnake.

My beloved steed broke his leg during the fall, and I was forced to give him a merciful death. The event made us decide to camp in the wooded area for the night, thinking we might be able to grab the runaway horse, but knowing another clan was nearby and lost him made us search out a camp.

That the Blackheart orcs had the female from the eatery was surprising. Did they come upon her ghost town also and she fed them? But instead of leaving, they dragged her off as a prize? I shouldn't care, it doesn't concern me, but seeing her tied and forced to make food with her hands bound angered us all.

"You want her so bad?" the Blackheart says in Orcish. "Then you'll fight with her, and we'll see who gets her when she's gutted between us. Perhaps we'll both take half, aye? I'd prefer the bottom, but I'm not picky. Her bottomless mouth will also do."

Even though my heart jumps, I keep my voice neutral. "And good for you if she's gutted. She won't bite off your brat-sized cock."

The female shrieks as he suddenly tosses her my way. I shove her behind me just as he jumps, all raw strength despite his weaker muscle tone. This orc has lived a good life, full of rich breads and butters. But there is immense strength beneath the layer of thick fat. He moves steadily and surefooted, his movements precise as I parry, careful to keep him where he can't reach the fallen female.

His beefy forearm brings the hunting knife down across my eye, but it's a move I'm familiar with—one that I'd nearly missed a decade ago if the scar over my brow and cheekbone is any indication. I deflect the blade by falling to the side at the same time I strike the soft flesh of his open underarm. He roars in agony and before he can strike again, I pull a dick move.

My boot in his balls.

It's a dirty maneuver, but I have no other choice, not with the female behind me scrabbling to get away from the fierce fighting. She's probably afraid I'll fall and crush her beneath me.

She has no idea she's supposed to stay put.

"Be still," I command her in a hiss. I don't want to pull her to the front of me and fight with one arm; she's safer behind the width of my back.

But the hellcat screeches and scrambles to run, even on all fours, as the Blackheart throws himself at me. It seems I won't be able to get away with keeping her safe.

I jab him in the throat at the same time I stick my foot behind me to trip her. When he chokes, I grab her by the arm and clasp her to the front of me like a shield. Her skirts rip as I fasten her legs around my waist and whisper into her ear.

"Hold on tight if you want to live."

Her eyes grow wildly large and distrustful. Why? She was fine in the eatery but now she wants nothing to do with orcs of any kind. A small part of me hoped she would be fine with us should our paths ever cross again. This male has ruined her for all orcs.

The male raises his blade, intending to shove it through her back now that she's exposed.

A rush of fury roils up my spine as I crush her to me and whip my blade across his jugular. Blood explodes from the gash, drenching both me and the girl in the instant red shower.

He collapses at our feet with a thundering roar and then there's dead silence.

Joanna:

Oh, God. The scarred orc from the eatery realizes he left gold in the pouch, not coppers. He came back for his coin purse—probably got the bags mixed up—and intends to leave me here with the orcs.

That's the last thought that crosses my mind before he jerks me to him, crushing my ribs in the process, and stabs the orc—which I realize once the hot spray of blood splashes across my back.

It immediately soaks in, from the back of my skull down to my bum—warm, wet blood—living blood, a life force. And the vessel that it purged from drops like a tree at my feet. My horrified eyes fly up to the scarred orc to see the wash of blood across his face too.

"Did they take your coin, *m'kirn*?" he rumbles.

Aye, it is as I thought. He has returned for the pouch.

"N-no," I whisper. "He didn't yet have a chance." A drop of blood falls from the top of my head and trickles down my forehead like macabre rain.

"We will bathe in the river," he says to the pretty one, that unscarred leader of his. The other nods and begins barking something in their language at the unfriendly orcs. The two scramble, the one who'd previously claimed Pegasus heading toward him, but I screech out—brave as can be— "That's my horse."

The unscarred leader barks at them again and they sullenly return to the body of their fallen friend. That's the last thing I see before the scarred orc carries me toward the creek.

He plunges us in, clothes and all, and my legs fall away from his waist as the sodden garments take weight.

"Female clothes are heavy," he says, placing a hand on top of my head to dunk me.

I come up sputtering and he dunks me again, merciless with his prize. It could be worse. He could be yanking off my clothes like the last orc tried. He spins me around and scrubs at the back of my dress, brings my skirts up to rub. I wait for his hands to fall lower, to slap my arse even, but he never strays there. His hands are huge as he rubs the garment only, and I try to tell myself that even though he's given me sore ribs, he probably doesn't mean to. He just doesn't know his own strength.

I hope.

I pretend that he's good inside and that he's rescued me because he wants to.

Because there's something about this scarred, ugly brute. He's not conventionally handsome, not like his leader friend. But he's handsome inside, if it makes any sense. He's gruff, grumpy, growly, and harsh. But not evil. Not like the sharp tusked evil grin of the one he slaughtered. The one who had enjoyed beating his own friend for the human toy. Not like the one who gleefully chose my horse over me, knowing he wouldn't have to tangle with one of the others.

I'm shivering now, the sun long gone, and I almost swear he pulls me closer to his body than necessary, but perhaps he's also patting me down for his coin purse. If my teeth would stop chattering, I'd just tell him it's in the cleavage between my breasts. I'd hoped the other orc would just flip up my skirts instead of ripping the entire gown down from the chest and I could hide it until one day I'd break away.

And now that I realize how close I came to the skirt flipping actually happening, my body starts to tremble. If these orcs hadn't come, I'd be suffering right now.

But I shut that part of my mind down. I refuse to think about it, just like the nights I had to endure Homer. Until a whore passed through Granby and slipped me some herbs from the mountain.

Made the male part of him go as soft as a rabbit.

The whore had looked at me with knowing eyes and I'd been embarrassed to think about what she might have heard the night before. But eternally grateful. And perhaps that wouldn't be such a bad occupation, if I could find another in Serenity, one who might teach me the ropes. Teach me about their teas for birth control, these herbs that can control a man's temper—and erection. If there isn't a seamstress position available.

The orc hauls me from the creek and uses his much larger palms to twist my skirts, wringing as much water as he can. I shiver as I hold the sodden dress up from getting muddy.

"You will remain untouched," he says, looking me over as if I displease him. "Take off the dress to dry."

I do it quickly, not because his voice is so growly, not because I'm afraid he'll rip it off himself if I pause, but because I don't want the coin purse to fall out and anger him further. To remind him of his mistake.

He barely looks at me as he takes the dress from my trembling white hand and gives it one more good wringing, then drapes it over a branch. He removes his tunic, which fits tight, the sleeves barely fitting around the obscenely bulging of bicep muscles. If we were alone, I'd offer to split the seams and stitch them into seamed V's.

But I don't.

He removes his leathers, and I have to avert my eyes from the huge swinging dick. And then, like I'm a doll, he picks me up and heads back toward the camp site. I'm okay with curling into his massive chest because he's warm and well, he washed me instead of attacking me.

The body has been hauled away and the two orcs are tied together, back-to-back. Their ankles are bound and there's a guard watching them.

"Wh-what's your name?" I ask the scarred one.

"Latsil."

"I'm Joanna."

"Hmm." Latsil grunts. Then after a few moments, he says, "that one is Kreele. Over there is Terk. Our prince is Brun. That one is Azorr. And the one keeping guard is Gorvan."

Terk wiggles his fingers at me, and Kreele nods his head. Gorvan hisses, showing me his tusks, before turning back to watch the prisoners.

"What will your prince do with them?" I ask as he lays me down on the dead man's furs.

He curls up next to me, his large body warm as the fire crackles just beyond us. My thin slip is already dry.

"They are free to leave in the morning when we leave. They will return to their clan with the news that their leader lost his life in a challenge. Now, try to get some rest, *m'kirn*. It will be a busy morn."

I'd like to ask why he challenged for me, but I'm afraid the other orcs are listening. I'm sure he doesn't want to admit to the coin that I hold. I'm determined to stay awake and think all these things through, but the prince has lain down and Kreele is staring drowsily at the fire. I'm warm and safe and exhausted.

The camp stirs to life with the first dawn's rays. I come awake to find Latsil staring at me. Of course, he is, I guess I'm lucky he hasn't rummaged in my slip for his coin.

"Come," he growls. "We shall get dressed."

If there was any moment of warmth last night, it's gone in the early light of day. He's brusque and short tempered as I follow him to the tree where our clothes have dried during the night.

I wring my hands as I pull my dress over my underthings, the bulge between my breasts weighing heavily. "Do you wish your coin back?" I ask.

"What?! No." He scowls as if I gave him the ultimate insult. "That was payment for our meal."

"It was too much," I whisper, afraid he's still unaware that it was gold instead of copper.

"Female. It was given freely," he all but barks and I find myself cowering, which makes him scowl even more. I stay out of his way after that, watching as they send the two orcs that had been bound on their merry way. They seem grateful enough, having two horses to ride away on. I'm not sure what happened to their third, but it seems to be missing along with the dead one's body.

Brun watches me carefully. I'd noticed him earlier, watching Latsil. He's a watcher, apparently.

"They only had two horses. One of them admitted to setting his free, thinking he would claim yours. He thought if he already had his own, Ufring, the dead ringleader, would take his horse like he claimed you. He's happy as a bandit to get to claim Ufring's steed. Apparently, it was finer than his."

I'm not sure how to answer him.

"Do you have any bags?"

"No. I left right after you all did, just grabbed the horse and ran."

His dark eyes watch me shrewdly, but he doesn't ask more than that.

"Do you mind riding with Latsil? We stopped here because he lost his steed. Rattlesnake scared him."

"Oh no! I'm so sorry about that. Of course, I don't mind riding with him." After all, they could just take my horse. It's what the last orcs were going to do. Maybe that's why Latsil is so crabby. The poor man just lost his horse.

"We will take you with us to Solaya. It's the gateway to our home, well protected and normally humans aren't allowed."

Interesting that he acts like he's doing me a favor. I guess maybe these orcs are different than the last.

I nod.

After the camp is packed up, I come upon Latsil bribing Pegasus with the last apple.

"I hear you need a ride," I say softly.

A grunt is my response.

"I'm sorry about your horse."

"Midnight was the twin of Darkness, Brun's steed. A very rare occurrence for both foals to survive birth."

With those simple words, I know how much he's hurting. I reach out to touch him and forget he's practically sleeveless until my hand touches bare skin.

He's warm. And so hard, all muscles, no fat. I suck in a breath of early morning air and hope it cools the odd feeling that's left me confused.

"I'm sorry. I know you'll miss him."

"It means I'll be forced to remain in Solaya on guard duty. I can't ride with the others."

"Mount up!" Brun calls and the rest of them hop onto their animals.

I stand around awkwardly, but Latsil calmly reaches out and wraps his huge hands around my waist to lift me. I swing my leg over Pegasus and feel his weight settle behind me. Large, muscled thighs wrap around me, and I can't help but feel... connected? It's probably because we slept so intimately together during the night, with him naked, and with me, with nothing but my thin undergarments between us.

With him this close, with his arms wrapped around me, he handles the reins and I'm fine with that. He's used to a horse and while I've only ridden Pegasus once, I imagine Midnight was the same size of majestic beast.

Halfway through the ride, I find myself slumping against Latsil's chest. He doesn't seem to mind, whispering into my ear as if it's handy to have me in this position.

"What will you do with me when we get to Solaya?" I ask.

"You will serve."

"Serve?"

"Aye. You served males at your eatery. You served the male orcs in the woods. Now you will serve our whores. It will be much easier, aye?"

Chapter Three

*J*oanna:

I've never seen so many boobs in my life.

Doesn't matter that they're green, albeit various shades. Gray green. Yellow green. Brown green. Spring green. Green, green, green.

My favorites are the larger nipples, circled by deeper green areolas. They just kind of pop. Second favorite is what I call the tipped boobies. The entire areola and nipple look like one piece, a whole pointed tip of a boob. Fascinating. The small boobs are pretty too, actually. Delicate and petite. But this orc woman's boobs? They're perfect. Round, jutting forward, just the right amount of bounce and no sag to speak of.

"Are you staring at my titties?" Demands the orc woman I'm serving.

I gulp and tear my eyes away from her boobs to focus on her face. She has a gold ring in her septum and the longest eyelashes I've ever seen. Most orcs have brown or black hair but hers is dark, so dark, and tinged with green highlights. Her lips are full and pouty, and she has a dimple in each of her cheeks.

Her face is quite pretty too. A fact that I didn't notice because she's right... I was staring at her titties.

"I don't swing that way," she goes on. "But maybe my girl, Grunalda does."

"Do not," another orc woman says, passing by but stopping long enough to talk. "Though she's pretty enough. I guess I could do her. With enough ale." She leans forward and... sniffs.

Sniffs my hair.

I take a step forward, but I'm trapped between the two.

"Uh... I think I'm fine. Sorry," I babble to the first one. "I'm a little shorter than you and at eye level with your... um... your... bouncy baubles."

Both orc women stare at me with wide eyes, and then they die laughing. Though I'm purposefully *not* looking, I still can't help but notice the perfect amount of bounce.

"Bess... did she call them bouncing bubbles?" The one from behind me steps up, crowding us both.

"Baubles," the first one corrects, wiping her eyes. "I think we should have gotten to know humans before this. Take her under our wing." Her voice changes, the depth snarling like the male orcs do. "Vin! Get your ass out here."

"What the hell now?" A third woman comes out of a tent a short distance away, then stops when she sees me cocooned between them. "What is that?"

"A human. From the village beyond. She was picked up by Prince Brun's team and told to serve. But methinks she's fascinated with the ladies." The second orc—the one who offered to do me if she had enough ale—peers at me. "Aren't you?"

"Um... no, actually. I'm not."

The third orc doesn't even hear me. "Fascinated with females? Then what the hell did you call me out here for? I thought the hunting party was back." She scratches her big ass, right in front of me, not ladylike at all.

"Who told you to serve?" The pretty one, Bess, asks.

"L-Latsil."

Bess gives a pointed look to Vin, and Vin gives the look over to Grunalda.

The three of them seem to pass a secret among them.

"Latsil, eh. Well, sit right here, human. I'm Bessica. This is Grunalda. And Vinshesa is the hungover tramp." Warily, I take the chair Bessica pushes toward me with her foot.

"I have the beginnings of a cold," Vinshesa sniffs.

"She's a lush," Grunalda mouths.

"Whore!" Vinshesa screeches at Grunalda.

Grunalda casually shrugs, the movement makes her nipples poke through the thin garment she wears. "'Tis true."

She takes a chair to sit in, then casually lifts her tank top up over her head and leans back to get the sun's rays over her naked boobs.

I gulp and look away, but not before noticing Bessica watching me.

"I'm Joanna," I say, and it comes out in a whisper.

"Lady dabbler?" Vinshesa asks her and jerks her head toward me.

"She insists not. I guess she can prove it. Once the hunting party arrives, we shall see which one she's interested in."

"None. I'm not interested in men." Oops, that didn't come out right. They might push off Grunalda on me. "I mean, I'm not interested in a *relationship*."

The three women burst into sudden laughter.

"Aye, little one. Don't fret. No one asked you for a relationship," Vinshesa sneers. "We merely asked if you would spread your legs. Male, female. Neither matters to us."

"S-spread my legs?" I gulp. "No. I was told I'd serve."

I mean, maybe the orc males meant I'd serve sexually? Maybe I'd misunderstood? I thought they said I'd serve the whores... meaning I'd fetch their food. Stuff like that. Took me a whole week to figure out that whores are held in high esteem in the orc clans. In what other culture would a species provide servants for them? And from what I gathered, not everyone can be a whore. In fact, I've been meaning to ask how one steps up from servant to whore... and exactly what the nighttime details entail. I mean, if I can demand enough gold for my services, maybe I don't have to put out much. Maybe I can just moan a couple times and be done.

"I kind of like her," Vinshesa says. "Tell us how you met Latsil."

Again, with this Latsil. Who is he? I mean, he was nice enough. Considering how brutal he looked—his scarred lip, his jagged ear, the constant scowl.

"He was the one who rescued me," I begin. "Your prince—"

"Brun," Bessica says.

"Brun. He told me he'd bring me here and I'd serve. And they'd talk to me when they got back from the hunt."

"Where did they rescue you?" Grunalda asks, sitting up in her seat.

"The Blackheart Orcs."

The three women immediately somber.

I should tell them their clan didn't exactly have a choice in my rescue. But I don't.

"And what did you think of Latsil?"

The question makes me blink. "I-I didn't really pay attention. I don't think he liked me much."

"Why not?"

"I don't know. Because he didn't say a whole lot? He just grunted, picked me up, and carted me away."

"Any of the Blackhearts come after you?"

I nod, remembering the gory scene. "He ripped him to shreds." With me in his arms. I can still remember the warm blood that sprayed across me.

"Then he likes you," Vinshesa says.

"What? No. You're wrong."

"Nay, I'm not. If he didn't care for you, he would have ripped *you* to shreds, little Joanna."

A round of cheers echoes around the village as huge clouds of dust stir in the outer distance beyond the stone pillars that serve as gates. The sounds of galloping horses fill the air, just like two weeks ago. Except, two weeks ago I was riding on the horse with Latsil, right before he dumped me off here.

Now, they're back, the same orcs who left me here in their village weeks ago have stopped inside the open gates.

Latsil jumps off his steed while another man takes the reins and leads the animal away. Latsil stands there, proud as can be, and he looks about the village.

"The return of the hunting crew," Bessica says, standing up. "Come along, Joanna. We must greet the warriors with a kiss."

"Huh?"

"It is custom," Grunalda says. "Hurry, before the lines grow."

But we don't have to worry about the line leading to Latsil. His dark eyes, rimmed with kohl, glitter as he looks around the camp, and then he freezes when they land on me. His lips curl into a sneer. I knew it. I knew he didn't like me.

Time stops still as Bessica grabs me by the hand and pulls me along with them. When we reach the entry, Latsil takes long-legged strides to meet us.

And then, right there where I stand with Bessica on one side and Grunalda and Vinshesa on the other, he drops down to one knee.

Icy cold dread permeates my belly, freezing my innards and making my heart pound harder.

Is he about to propose?

Oh, horror of horrors, I don't want that. I never want that, no matter if he's a stranger or not. If I refuse, they may toss me out of the camp. If I say yes, they'll hear the lie, see the quiver in my lips before I burst into uncontrollable sobs at being resigned to the same fate I'd once escaped from. I'm an ungrateful wench for even considering saying no since they rescued me from a fate worse than death.

"Kiss him!" Grunalda whispers, harshly knocking against my shoulder with hers.

I stare at her in confusion, and she makes a puckering motion with her lips. Horrified, I look to the right to see the other two motioning toward Latsil and puckering too, kissing the air silently.

And then I notice all the other warriors who arrived with him are getting hugs and kisses. I'm more lost than ever as to what's going on, but, well, I'll roll with it. Maybe explain later that I don't really want a marriage. Maybe he'll undo it.

I lean forward, my hands on his strong shoulders, noting his skin feels slightly damp with sweat. I don't mind it; he smells good. Manly.

I deposit a kiss right onto his lips. His tusks press against the sides of my mouth, and I can feel his breath hitch. Behind me, the girls are quiet as church mice.

Too quiet.

I pull away from Latsil to see the three of them staring in shocked horror. In fact, Latsil looks downright stunned too.

"Not on the lips," Grunalda says. "Or, I guess, you can if you want to. But that's a lot of males to be kissing."

Now she tells me.

"Huh. Maybe she's *not* into females," Bessica whispers to Vinshesa. "Too bad, Grun."

"Shut up."

"She doesn't know our ways," Latsil growls, staring at the three orc women like it's their fault I'm so clueless, when he was the one who dumped me in the middle of camp to find my own way around. "You three should teach her our customs."

"Oh, we'll teach her all right," Vinshesa says, glaring at Latsil. "Joanna, I don't think you were meant to serve others. Do you wish to become a whore like us? It is the greatest career in the village."

Oh, God's Fire, this is my chance to squirm out of his odd marriage proposal?

"I do," I say quickly. "I do want to become a whore." I mean, it's a paid position, isn't it?

"A new one?" Another male asks, eyeing me curiously, stepping up to where we stand.

Latsil suddenly bristles. "She is in training! Do not even look at her for at least three moons."

The other orc looks curious, then slaps him on the shoulder, turns and leaves.

Again, I'm still confused as to all these strange customs, but I feel strangely satisfied. I think accepting the position just pulled me out of the proposal territory. And why the huge orc would want me—other than I'm a novelty—is beyond me.

Bessica looks thoughtful. "We will train her. She will be the best whore ever."

Said no one ever. And least not where I come from.

Chapter Four

L *atsil:*

She wishes to be a whore.

Other males eye her appreciatively and I know she won't have a lack of attention. Something inside me boils at the thought of someone else with her. I imagine her full lips pursed for another male, her eyelashes sweeping lazily over her eyes in the throes of lust, and I want to beat my fists against the wall. I want to pound any male who dares to touch her.

I have three moons to get her out of my system before she ruins me. I can never live it down if I fall for yet another female.

"What ails you?" Bessica asks, startling me.

I scowl my frustration with her. Sneaky orc, coming up upon me. "Nothing ails me! Why are you here?"

She shrugs easily. "To see which whore you prefer."

"I don't need any whores." I bring the axe down over the wood I'm splitting.

"Still carrying a grudge?" she asks.

Meddlesome orc. "Of course not. It was a long time ago."

"She still feels bad."

"What's done is done." I just want this conversation ended, though, for the first time, I realize it isn't as painful as it would have been six moons earlier. It seems I am finally getting over my broken heart.

It's been years.

"Well, if you're over it, I could use someone to help rear Joanna. Unless you'd rather I ask Kreele."

"Kreele won't touch her," I snap. He knows my turmoil regarding Joanna, the entire crew who ate at her diner in Granby does.

Her eyes light with interest. "Oh?"

Just like that, she has something to latch onto.

And then I sigh. "Fine, I'll help with Joanna." Because that will be the easiest way to squelch any rumors that are flying from when I gave her my gold purse during our excursion.

Bessica leans back with a smirk on her face. For the first time, I notice how lovely my friend's little sister has grown up to be. And while she may look like a fine orcen female, she's still a bratty busybody.

A busybody who allowed her best friends to kill my mate.

Did Tavri deserve it? Yes. But that doesn't change the fact that it ripped my heart in two. I stomp off to the main hut, Bessica on my heels, to find the human who can't stop serving everyone. The kitchen orcs love her; the male orcs love her, and now? It seems even the whores love her.

The whole idea makes me scowl. I'm aware of my sour mood as I round the corner to find my males sitting around a table drinking ale. As if Bessica is waiting for my reaction, she moves to stand behind her brother, Kreele, and rubs his shoulders as she watches me.

I flag down Joanna and because I have to do so, I can't help but bark at her. "Bring me a tankard of ale."

She blinks and then hurries to the kitchen to fetch it.

I hear Kreele laugh at something Bessica whispers and it makes my mood sink to even more churlish standards.

When Joanna returns with a large tankard poured so full it threatens to slosh, she also carries a plate of fruit to snack on. She places both on the table in front of me.

I didn't ask for anything to nibble on. She must have assumed I was hungry. How dare she act as if she knows me?

"Come sit," I command and don't give her a chance to say no. I'm well aware that I'm not the prettiest male to look at, especially since I'm always near Brun which makes me a hundred times uglier.

A fact that my previous mate let me know often. One of the many reasons Bessica tripped her or pulled her hair. One of the many reasons I'd yell at her, and it would cause Kreele and me to fight.

But even Kreele comforted me after Tavri's death.

All the males did. For three days straight, we sat and drank tankards of ale in silence until we passed out from the pain.

"Umm," Joanna says, looking around like she wishes to make an excuse not to sit near me.

"I didn't ask," I say, yanking the fragile wrist toward me until she falls into my lap.

Her wide eyes find Bessica as if she isn't sure what to do... yet she is worried about disrupting her new status. Bessica mimes feeding a male and Joanna gulps.

Is it really that abhorrent to be my whore, then?

I'm surprised when, instead of picking up a piece of fruit to feed me with, Joanna smooths out the scowl smashed into my forehead. Her small, delicate fingers are cool and smooth on my brow.

"What's wrong, Latsil?" she whispers. "Don't you feel well?"

It seems like the entire table grows quiet, waiting for my response. I can't help but drop my voice to match hers, and at the last minute I realize it sounds intimate for us to huddle together to whisper.

"You aren't going to simply assume the way to a male's heart is through his stomach?"

"Nay," she says and would have said more if Kreele doesn't cut in.

"The orc sulks like a brat because he won't be included in the trip next full moon. We're going back to Serenity to pick up Brun's bride."

"First time they'll go without me," I admit, flashing a dirty look to Kreele.

"Why aren't you going?" Joanna demands and *glares* at Brun like he's committed a grievous offense.

Again, Kreele chuckles.

Brun holds up his hands toward her. "Not my fault. There isn't an available steed for him. If there are any for sale we will buy one. Otherwise, he must stick around near the village to see if any feral herds run by so he can find one to break in—"

"You're not going because you don't have a horse?" Joanna asks me.

I give a short nod, not understanding why she's so surprised. Surely, she's never seen two orcs riding together on a steed? We'd break the beast's back, for sure.

"Aww, Latsil. Sweet," she whispers, and someone grunts under his breath that she dares to call me sweet. No one is aware that the time I spent with her is probably the sweetest I've ever been. "You don't have to worry about that. You can have Pegasus."

My jaw drops and there is dead silence around the table.

Finally, Bessica speaks. "Jo-Jo... not sure if you understand that a whore gets paid. Not the other way around."

I can't help but bring her hand up to my ugly, scarred mouth—the mouth that has no right to touch such perfect skin—and kiss her fingers.

"Thank you, *m'kirn*. I can't accept such an expensive beast."

She frowns. "Why not? You need a horse. I have a horse. I give him to you."

As I shake my head, she turns to Brun—the same Brun she scowled at so fiercely earlier. "Can't he accept?"

Brun inclines his head. "He can. But if you don't choose to stay?"

She shrugs. "Then I'll beg a ride to a town somewhere. I'll figure out something."

I'm gentle when I grip her chin and turn her focus back to me. "Any time you need a ride anywhere, you come to me, Joanna. You hear?"

Silly female has a smile as wide as me when she nods. And then, with everyone watching, she remembers to act like a whore and plops a berry into my mouth. When a drop of juice runs down the scarred recess of my bottom lip, she catches it with her finger—and then licks it clean.

Licks. It. Clean.

Just like that, my bad mood clears. Ten minutes with Joanna and my mood is elevated to that of a young orcling whose balls have just dropped.

This is a warning sign for everyone present... because everyone knows of my shameful past.

It is why I can never mate again, so it may be best that Joanna is a whore.

Joanna:

I'm not sure why this orc refuses to let me love him. In the literal sense, of course. Though, if I'm honest, he's someone I could love emotionally. There's something broken about him that tears at my heartstrings. Knowing that he loved his horse, that Midnight was his family and especially connected because he was the sibling to Brun's horse. As far as I can tell, Latsil has no family other than his best friend, Brun.

Bessica gave me lessons on how to please Latsil... and I'm not sure I want to know how she knows. Grunalda took pity on me and told me in private that Bessica grew up with Brun, Latsil, and the rest of the bunch. Her brother, Kreele, ran with them so she was the little sister always in the way.

For now, I continue to feed Latsil berries, trailing my finger into his mouth with each one and letting him suck my fingertip clean. The pull his suckling does makes waves of heat pool between my legs. I'm not sure that the whore is supposed to feel this much for an individual orc but for now, until I get the hang of things, Latsil is the only one who'll have access to me.

One day I'll be a full-fledged whore. Not today. And right now, sitting on his lap, feeling the hard muscles underneath my bum, I don't mind one whit that he's it for me until then. I'm going to enjoy every minute of his surliness. You'd think I'd need a happy man after all that I've been through, but apparently not. I seem to crave brooding orcs instead.

I splay my palm onto his chest and feel the deep rhythm of his heartbeat. It pounds faster with my touch, but mayhap that is wishful thinking on my part.

"Joanna, are you sure you wish to be a whore? You know you'll have to service ugly mugs like this one, right?" Terk asks.

Latsil picks up a carrot and pitches it at Terk.

"Don't listen to him, *m'kirn*. He's jealous," Latsil whispers as if soothing me.

Terk's words, though I know he teases, make me angry.

"You forget I've seen what's below the belt," I whisper sultrily. "And it's big and beautiful."

The orcs look stunned by my response.

"Son of a bitch," Terk says.

Grunalda whoops and Bessica starts laughing.

"She'll be the best ever," Vinshesa says.

When the laughter dies down, the ale flows more freely. But I'm aware that Latsil limits himself.

"Where do you sleep *m'kirn*?" he asks.

"I bunk in the cabin with the kitchen help."

"You'll sleep with me tonight," he says. And then he fingers the frayed neckline of my dress. "We'll need to get you some more clothes."

"I can make my own," I say. "I'll just need to visit a village with fabrics and sewing supplies I can purchase."

"We shall go visit the next two towns."

"Aye, I promised we'd be back to escort Anna, Mabel, and Beth," Brun says from across the table. "We can all head out at first light."

And I shall buy enough fabric and thread that I won't have to leave this orc village for a while. Because quite frankly it's more wonderful than any human village I've lived in. I toiled all day on my daddy's farm and then spent evenings helping momma with the sewing.

One thing the lady-whores haven't taught me was... what to do when the orc you're taking care of starts taking care of you instead. Latsil starts giving me sips of his ale and as soon as I get giddy inside, he starts nibbling it off my lips. I forget all about being a whore and start kissing him back, licking the scar that bisects his lips, wishing I'd have been there to care for him when he was cut. I can't help but giggle as I whisper against his broken ear that I liked riding with him on the horse. I liked the way his strong thighs butted up to mine, I liked the way his arms came around me to reach the reins.

"Mmm, liked that did ye, pretty thing?" he rasps, his breath hot against the side of my neck.

"Very much," I agree happily, suddenly squinting. The sun has gone down without me even noticing and just the flames of the firepit light the night.

I turn sideways in his lap and trace my lips over his shoulder where the scar there is smoother. I kiss it, aware that he's still as a statue. "Why do you have so many more than the others?" I ask.

"Does it bother you?" There's a dark tone to his voice, but I'm too sotted to figure out why.

"Nope. Just makes you tougher than any of them."

"My scars are not honorable, *m'kirn*," he whispers near my ear.

For some reason, that tone penetrates, and I stare at him with my brows knotted.

"Let's get you tucked in, shall we?" he murmurs, picking me up as easily as he would a feather.

But tucked in is exactly what he means.

He has a tent set up in Solaya, like the other male riders do. From what I understand, they mostly live in the mountains less than a day's ride from us. As soon as we enter his tent, he tenderly plucks at the laces of my gown, and I shiver when his fingertip brushes against my stiffened nipple.

It's not a surprise to find he has to work his breeches off over his swollen cock. But then, with both of us naked as the day we were born, he pulls me tight to him and wraps the furs around us.

And wakes me the next morn.

Chapter Five

Joanna:

I'm baffled when I sneak into Bessica's tent for my pack. In it is my coin purse of gold, which I'll need for shopping.

Latsil's lips had tightened when I told him I had to head to Bess's tent for my stuff. He doesn't like that my belongings are stored elsewhere. It's not like I can walk around the camp all day carrying my pack, which contains all the belongings I own; the sole pot, my canteen, and the empty bag of apples I'd taken from the stables.

"Bess," I hiss at the flap over the door.

"Come in," she grumbles sleepily. "For such a little pipsqueak, you have the loudest mouth."

"Mayhap you just drank too much ale last night," I mumble as I enter her tent... and freeze. There's a man in her bed and both are as naked as the day is long.

"Is she blushing?" Terk asks. "How far in her whore's training did she get?"

"Oh, shush," Bess says, wiggling her ass against his crotch. "You know that's lady business."

"Sorry to bother you," I say, heading to the wooden chest of drawers that houses my stuff.

"How did it go with Latsil last night?" Bessica asks. "Did you remember to use lots of tongue on him? He loves to be worshipped."

I'm sure my cheeks are still burning as I admit the godawful truth. "No. We didn't do anything. He tucked me into bed like nothing happened out at the campfire. Like we never shared any kisses or sweet words or anything. I must've done something wrong." I can't help but wring my hands. "Maybe he finds me lacking."

Terk snorts. "He doesn't find you lacking, *m'kirn*. Just the opposite."

"Didn't you hear?" I grumble. "He didn't touch me."

"It's not you," he says, then turns to Bessica. "Didn't you tell her?"

"Nay," she scowls. "'Tis not my story to tell."

Terk barks out laughter, then nibbles her ear. "I've never seen you hold back gossip, sweet."

"What do you mean by that?" she asks, and blinks lazily. Even first thing in the morning, she's beautiful, like a ripe, lush goddess. "I can keep a secret with the best of them."

And that causes Terk to narrow his eyes at me. "Speaking of which, you are to tell no one you found me in here. Especially not Kreele. Got it?"

"Got it," I snap impatiently. "What story?"

Terk rolls out of bed, butt-naked, and I avert my eyes as I dig through my pack for my coin purse. He pulls on his pants as he says, "Humans don't know, but you're one of us now so I'm going to let you in on a little secret. When a male orc falls in love, it's a once in a lifetime love for him. It's why a lot of orc matings are arranged. A male can't be trusted to pick the right mate when he lives in the clouds. Unfortunately, Latsil didn't have anyone to arrange a mating for him."

I blink at that. Of all the things... I never expected that Latsil was already married, or as orcs say, mated.

I didn't think the whores were available for mated men. I guess I never thought to ask.

"She's dead," Bessica says simply, noticing the look on my face. "But it was such a bad mating, he's never recovered. Not wholly."

"He loved her that much?"

"Aye," Terk says. "'Tis not always good for an orc to love." I don't think it's my imagination that he looks at Bessica.

"But you'll help him heal," Bessica says. "You'll be his personal little healer. We'll show you exactly what he likes, and how to please him."

"Why?"

"Because he's one of ours," she says simply. "And he deserves it. He's a generous and kind soul. You watch and see."

Terk grunts and all at once I'm aware of the purse of gold in my bosom. I'd thought Latsil was grumpy but then I think back to when we ate at Homer's. He was grinning when I tore into my meal like there was no tomorrow. Almost like he knew I was being sneaky and enjoying my food. I think of the way he cuddled me during the night and the next day on the horse. Even last night. He may not have touched me the way a woman wants a man to touch her, but he held me while I slept off my drunken stupor.

There may be more to Latsil than I first thought. It makes sense why I found him so interesting. Why I wanted—want—to know his story.

"Are you ready to leave, Joanna? Perfect excuse for me to be seen leaving Bessica's tent is to walk you back."

"Aye. I have all my goods," I say wryly. Haven't yet used my cooking pot, nor my canteen.

He kisses Bessica goodbye, and he and I exit her tent. A couple of orcs wave at us and I can't quite believe he and Bessica keep their relationship from her brother.

"You're going to bathe before we leave, right?" I ask, wrinkling my nose.

Terk's tusks gleam as he chuckles. "Don't care for the sweaty smell of sex under the hot sun, *m'kirn*?"

"I feel bad for the horse," I tease.

"I'll dunk in the stream before we go," he says.

"Use soap."

He guffaws and hooks an arm around my neck. I'm about to protest about rubbing his scent on me when a roar jerks him away.

"I told you all she's off limits!" Latsil shouts, shoving him as I shriek.

Terk lands in a muddy puddle, looks up at us and narrows his eyes. "For how long, Lats?" he whispers.

The somber tone makes Latsil calm down. "Three full moons," he says, his voice normal again as if he realizes he might have been out of hand.

"Aye." Terk nods and Latsil grabs my arm, hauling me quickly down the path. I look back over my shoulder at Terk, who winks. At least he has an excuse to jump in the creek, I guess.

"You're hurting me," I snap, yanking my arm from his grip.

Latsil turns to me and looks surprised, then sorry. "Stay away from them, Joanna. You're not trained for orcs. You must be broken in gently, stretched, wet and completely willing. You can't just jump in the furs with anyone who flirts."

Is he jealous or exerting his power as a trainer? I can't help but feel a little okay with that. Before I can respond, he speaks again.

"Why do you wish to be a whore anyway? I set you to serve—"

"Every man I know has put me to serve in some way, shape or form. But being a whore—it means I can't get mated or married, right?"

"Aye. For the most part. Unless someone, your parents or an elder has the right to arrange with another a mating for you."

"Well, that keeps me safe. No parents here, right?"

The corner of his crooked lip turns up. "Same. My parents were killed in orc wars."

"I never want to get married," I say. "Not that I think it would be legal anyway, since I already am."

His brows jump up. "You are?"

I nod. "I left him in hiding at the diner. You'd given me coin and I knew Homer would take it and I didn't feel like sharing, nor did I feel like having a husband. So, I grabbed Pegasus and fled. I thought I'd make it to Serenity, but the Blackhearts caught me."

"That's why you have nothing."

"I have much more than that. I have coin and I have freedom and I have safety." I sidle up to him and wrap my arms around his waist, then rub my cheek to his chest. He smells so good, like clean soap. "The day orcs were greeted at the village with a kiss, when you kneeled before me, I thought you were proposing. It's how humans do it, falling to one knee. It terrified me to have to turn you down."

He chuckles, though it's an empty sound. "You were afraid while you were married?"

"Terrified," I admit for the first time ever. "I never want to be married again."

"You will never be scared again, Joanna," he says, tipping my chin up to look into my face. "I will build you a cabin. I want you to have a place of your own, a place where you can always feel safe."

Gah. This brute is the sweetest orc in all the land.

By the time everyone has mounted their horses and we're on the way to Creede, his arms are around me.

I feel like I'm in seventh heaven. The sturdy muscles of Pegasus's gait below me, the warmth of the breeze blowing across my face, the strong arms wrapped around me reaching the reins, and the growly voice that whispers in my ear like we're the only two in the world all make for the perfect mood.

I think this is my favorite place to be. Maybe it's because I know that these rides are few and far between with Latsil. Most of his trips will be dangerous orc business, whatever business it is that orcs do. In the past I might have said pillaging, but their clan is different from the Blackhearts who attacked my village. Despite any dangers, I'll treasure each and every trip I'm allowed to take with this amazing man.

It gives me the strength and the courage to ask him what's been bothering me.

"Why didn't you touch me last night?"

Instead of answering the question, he asks one of his own in a deep, growly voice.

"Did you want me to?"

I'm not sure how to answer that. Surely, he knows?

"Um, yes?" I'm aware that I phrased my response as a question, and he gives a dark chuckle in my ear.

"*Cara'jek*"—it's not the usual phrase he uses. I'll have to remember to ask one of the others what it means— "when I touch you, it will be when you have full command of your senses. I don't want your judgment impaired in any way. I want you to be able to say yes or no."

It's that easy?

"Yes," I say happily. "I don't even care if we're out in the open and the others surround us."

"I'm sure we can find some privacy somewhere," he rumbles and that deep sound shoots sparks straight down me.

"It won't be like it was with your human husband," he warns suddenly.

"God, I hope not."

I'm rewarded with another rich chuckle.

I'm a little bit hesitant when I ask, "Have you ever been married? I mean, mated?"

I hold my breath, wondering if it was too bold to ask. Wondering if he'll answer in truth, or if he'll refuse.

"Yes," he admits finally.

"Did you leave her? Like I left my husband?" My questions rush out hurriedly, not wanting him to know that I've heard some of the story.

"Nay. She's dead."

"I'm sorry," I murmur.

"I was too, at first. I loved her. And I didn't care for how her death occurred. But I know now that it was necessary and I'm ready to forgive the way it happened."

He's quiet and I let those words sink in, wondering how I can ask for more information. Surely, he'd share more if he wanted to? But it seems like he's trying to phrase how to do that when he continues speaking.

"Vinshesa petitioned our king for allowance into our mating. We became a threesome."

"Is that done?" I ask, horrified. I can't imagine being happily mated and the king designates another person to enter. I can't believe Vin was mated to Latsil and no one told me.

"Not usually," he answers. "The king intervened, and my choice was to leave the clan if I didn't agree with his decision. Something inside me must have known this was a last resort. Vinshesa used the excuse that my mate hadn't gotten pregnant and that she was willing to be the one to continue our orc lines. Instead, she used her new power and status to kill Tavri."

I can't help the gasp that escapes my throat. Two shocks in a row, first finding out Vin was mated to Latsil and then finding out that she was a murderess. I guess I've always suspected there was something dark inside her, but I never would have known it was this deep.

"It was all planned out among the three whores. They knew that Vinshesa couldn't be punished for defending her mate, even when it was against another mate, so they gained entry into my mating by convincing King Brachard the genes of the largest orc must be carried on. That it would be beneficial for our clan. The worst punishment that could have happened to Vinshesa was that she be annulled from our mating. She was more than happy to become a whore again. It was what she wanted all along. So just when I wanted another mate to lean on, one to help me through the grief of losing the one I loved, instead she went on about her life as if she hadn't shattered mine."

"I-I'm so sorry." Confusion lines my voice. I'm really not sure how to feel about Vinshesa. If she is truly a drinker, like the other two tease her, there may be a reason. Maybe she's drowning her darkness, her murdering guilt, or maybe she feels more for Latsil than she admits.

"Are you sure she doesn't love you?" I ask.

"Nay, it is not like the love of a true mate. It has never been that way between us. She loves me in her own way, I imagine. We grew up together. It is more of the love you would carry for family. I know now that it must have cost her a lot to do this—to deprive me of both mates—more so than I realized at the time."

"Is it why she drinks?" I ask.

He sounds thoughtful when he says, "Aye. I didn't think of it before, but I would imagine so."

His arms tighten around me. "Maybe I should have listened more to Bessica when she tried to intervene. All I could see was my own misery."

I turn in his arms just enough to kiss his scarred cheek. "How could you not, Latsil? Be easy on yourself."

"You are too good to me, *m'kirn*."

"You are a good man, sir."

Chapter Six

Joanna:
    Creede is used to trading with orcs. It's a southern town, so I'd assume they haven't run into the Blackheart clan, which comes from the high north. But Latsil says when a town is known to trade with a certain clan, in this case the West Mountain Orcs, the Blackhearts keep their distance from them. It's sort of like unspoken protection for a village, I imagine. It makes me wonder what life would have been like if we'd been trading with these guys years ago, and why every human village doesn't welcome West Mountain with open arms. Mayhap my parents would still be alive, working on the farm.

    But then I shiver. Father had turned down Homer McLinn once for me, but would he have done so again? With no other prospects for me, and with him growing old? He must have known he could not keep up the farm forever and what would he do with no successor to care for him and mother as they grew older? I might be married to Homer right now anyway, working the farm myself because I can't see his round body sweating under the heat of the summer sun.

    We don't have to sleep on the trail tonight. We ride straight through to Creede because Latsil knew the hotel would accept orc guests and three whores. Well, four if you count me.

    The other three are human, which kind of surprised me. I mean, I knew human whores serviced the orcs, but it never dawned on me the orcs would make a trip out to pick them up and deliver them back to Solaya for safety.

It amazes me even more as I learn about these West Mountain orcs.

Anna, Mabel, and Beth aren't too different than me. A bit better dressed for sure, but none of them look down on me for being ragged. Instead, they seemed to know that sometimes a woman has nothing but the clothes on her back. Mabel tells Brun that she purchased a half carriage, which is like a normal carriage but without the top. It has wooden bench seats instead of fabric covered padding, built for necessity instead of comfort. She thought it would be good for the orcs because they could haul more supplies back to Solaya.

I find it interesting that she doesn't hesitate to gift something to the clan. She's not asking for kudos, or payment, or anything. She just thought it would be a good idea.

Latsil looks thoughtful as he considers the carriage. He says something to Brun in Orcish and Brun nods.

The group separates as we merge into the village market, with Brun and Mabel heading toward the stables where she has the carriage. Latsil takes me straight to the women's area, where he stands by my side, tall and proud, the only male in the section, which doesn't bother him one whit.

"I like this color," he comments, fingering a length of scarlet-dyed fabric. Not surprising, though he eyes the yellow unabashedly.

I will make a short piece of the scarlet to be worn in private in his tent then. Something sexy that hits below the hips but leaves my legs bare. Something that can be wrenched over my head in a hurry.

Hurriedly, I measure out the amount I'll need and I'm about to ask the price when Latsil pulls out his coin purse. I start to haggle price when I see he's willing to pay with gold.

"Lats," I hiss. "I have my own funds."

"Aye, *m'kirn*, I know," he responds easily. "I gave you those funds."

"To spend," I hiss, ignoring the grin of the matronly woman who sells the fabric. "Not to store."

She holds out her hand for the gold coin Latsil offers and I place mine over his.

"This one coin is enough to pay for the whole skein," I say, narrowing my eyes at the way she's willing to overcharge him.

"Nay, the dye is expensive," the woman argues.

I roll my eyes. "No proper, God-fearing woman will wear scarlet. You'll have this same fabric to sell next time," I chide. She can't fool a human the way she does the poor orcs.

"'Tis all right," Latsil says softly. "I have the funds, *m'kirn*."

I smile easily. "Then you should be charging her, milord. For we all know your presence keeps away the murderers and robbing types." I refuse to call them orcs, because we all know humans also rob villages, but orcs take all the blame.

Just like that the merchant smiles easier as she realizes she can't win.

"A fair price, milady," she whispers, even though we both know I am nothing more than a whore. "In exchange for you purchasing the rest of your wares at *my* table."

I give a quick glance at the other merchant tables. As expected, they all have the same fabrics she has, just with slight variances in the dye.

"Agreed," I say. "It saves us shopping time not having to dally at the other booths anyway."

Latsil flips two gold coins her way, way overpaying, but considering he was going to pay for one yard of fabric with a coin makes me decide to let it go.

"Give her anything she desires," he says to the merchant then turns to me. "*Cara'jek*, I have a small errand with Brun. Finish your shopping, I will be right back for you. Do not wander," he warns.

"She will be safe, sir," the merchant says as Latsil leans down to press his lips to my forehead. He wanders back to the male side of the trading post and the merchant and I watch his amazing, muscular form walk away.

"Your orc worries that others will convince you to return to the Lord," she says. "They usually seek out the lone females, especially the new ones."

"Considering I just left my marriage"—I give a sharp shudder—"there is nothing that could convince me to return."

She nods sympathetically. "I am lucky to have an honorable man. One who is fair and open minded toward all. That mentality has brought wealth and protection to our village."

"Wealth?" I look around at the dusty village. Despite having some charm, it does not look wealthy.

"We do not like to seek attention by flaunting it," she says, following my eye. "But our bellies are full, our children are happy, and our funds are hidden for emergencies."

"Smart move," I agree. "If my husband had been as wise as yours, my village might have fared better."

"Where did you come from, miss?" she asks, referring to me with a title that reflects my youth instead of my previous married state.

"Granby."

Her eyes widen.

"Are you the missing wife? Your husband was the leader, then? The mayor?"

"Aye," I acknowledge. "I did not have a choice in the marriage. During the last invasion, my parents were killed, and I was left alone. Homer proclaimed himself mayor and decided we would wed."

"'Tis rumored that orcs invaded a second time less than a moon ago and stole his new bride."

I roll my eyes. "And his horse too, I imagine?"

She giggles. "No mention of the steed in the rumor. How convenient, for a brave man would fight for his horse instead of his wife, eh?"

"Of course, he'd stay quiet about Pegasus," I say. "But the truth is I took an opportunity to run."

"He's already found another bride," she says. "Not one as young and pretty as you, but more worldly."

I tilt my head wondering what she gets at.

She leans in to whisper conspiratorially. "The vicar's wife."

I gasp. "What of the vicar?"

"She was of the peevish sort," the woman continues. "I imagine he was most relieved."

I can't help but giggle. Then the woman reaches beneath her table and pulls out more fabrics and sewing supplies.

"Take your pick," she says, as if she just realizes that what I said earlier was true. This orc clan does bring them protection and gold. They'd do well to keep them happy.

I stock up on so many fabrics that I begin to nibble my lip as she boxes them up. Scissors, needles, threads. Pins, tape, cushions. How in the world will we get all of this back? But then a huge green finger taps my bottom lip, making me release it from my bite.

"Latsil," I say, surprised that he snuck up without me hearing. "I may have overdone it."

"Nay, lass. It will fit," he says. "If not, we will buy our own half-carriage."

"I don't even know where I'm going to store all this stuff," I fret, hoping he'll offer a corner in his own tent until I figure this out.

He tilts my head up to meet his eyes. "*Cara'jek*, I told you I want you to feel safe. As soon as we get to Solaya, I will build you a cabin with room so you can sew. Until then, you can store your boxes in my tent. In fact, you can just stay with me in my tent. Keep it warm so I have something to look forward to when I return from the road, aye?"

I didn't quite believe he was serious when he said he'd build me a cabin. I don't need much, it can be as small as a tent, even smaller, it's just me.

"Are you sure?" I whisper.

His calloused finger sweeps the hair to tuck behind my ear. "Aye, beautiful. An ugly brute like me needs something lovely to brighten his home."

"You're not ugly." I frown, wondering if he really believes that. "You're big and strong. And your scars make you bad-ass. I don't care how you got them. They tell a story of what you've been through in your life." Because I can't help myself, I stand on my tiptoes and grab the back of his neck to pull him down toward me. When our lips come together, it's sweet and loving and everything it should be.

"You're my favorite orc in all the land," I confide.

His lips curl against mine. "You're my favorite human in all the land."

A throat clearing comes from behind us. Kreele grins. "My timing is perfect. The key to your room."

He flips it to Latsil, who catches it with a grunt.

The town of Creede boasts an outdoor shower. The merchant was right when she said their town was wealthy. The wealth equates to modern day conveniences so well hidden that pillagers won't know what to look for. When Kreele and Latsil carried the boxes to our hotel room, stacking them neatly in a corner, Kreele pointed out two robes laid on the bed. One was extra-large, orc sized. The other was human woman sized. I like that this town acknowledges the size difference with orcs.

Kreele walks with us back downstairs before he heads off to find the others. Latsil steers me to the back of the hotel. There is a huge wooden deck with about six showers. Each shower is enclosed with the privacy fence made of wood, with the feet and head area exposed. A large bucket is poised on top of each shower.

Latsil opens the door to one and ushers me into one of the stalls. He spins me around and unbuttons my dress, careful with his calluses as he brushes against my skin. When I step out of the dress, he drapes it on a hook just outside of the wooden barrier. I stand naked while he slowly strips.

I have never felt this comfortable with another. It doesn't bother me that he sees my body unclothed, and I love the way he looks at me with glittering eyes as if I'm the most precious thing on earth. When he's as naked as me, he pulls me close to him and brings us right under the bucket.

"Hold your breath," he says.

I look up to see that the shower head is somewhat different than I imagined. Instead of the bucket tipping to pour water onto a person, there's a false bottom that slides from it, revealing holes like a grate.

I suck in a deep breath and Latsil pulls the string that releases the bottom. Shock hits me when the water dumps on us. It sprays instead and is *heated*.

"What? How?" I splutter.

He chuckles. "The water is piped in from an underground spring. It is quite a sophisticated system. There is a bobble device inside the bucket, a sensor that notes when the water level is lower. More hot water is piped in to reach the previous levels."

"So, we'll never run out," I conclude.

"Precisely. We have the same system in Mont Grove, however, we do not have a heated spring to source it. We must first heat our water."

He takes a bar of soap and lathers his hands. I watch in utter fascination as the soap covers long thick fingers, and squared knuckles. He's so masculine it quickens my breath. He puts the bar back in the resting spot and slowly places both soapy palms on my breasts.

His gaze finds mine and we lock eyes before his large hands start rubbing the lather into my breasts. His thumbs roll over my hardened nipples and the pleasure zings through my body.

"Oh, Latsil," I murmur, my voice raspy.

"Like that?"

How can he doubt it? "Very much. And guess what?"

"What?" he asks, his thumbs continuing to rub erotically over my sensitive nipples.

"I have full command of every one of my senses."

"Then you want this, *cara'jek*?"

"I want you with every breath I take."

As if he still disbelieves, he moves his hand down to cup my sex, and his middle finger slides along the outside of my seam. He groans when he feels how slick I am for him.

"'Tis true," he murmurs, and the wonderment tears a little at my heart. Why does this man doubt that I wouldn't feel for him?

"Very true, milord," I whisper and then boldly grip his cock. It's absolutely beautiful, curved upward, thickly veined and a darker green.

He tosses his head back and groans, leaving me with the broad expanse of neck to see. It's probably the one area where he isn't scarred. And then as if we are both on track with the same idea, we hurriedly reach for the soap and start lathering our hands.

As soon as mine are lathered up, I rub them along every inch of him; his massive chest, his rippled abs, and then I take my time cleaning his cock. It's stiff and full in my hand and slowly I stroke it while using the other to soap his balls.

I need to reach for more soap to wash his heavy thighs, and I drop down to my knees to reach his calves and feet. He stands stock still as I kneel before him, and wickedly, I wonder if he imagines us in a bedroom with me kneeling before him, instead of covering him with soap.

Slowly I walk around him and start the entire process over again from the beginning, starting at the base of his neck. When he's covered in bubbles, he kneels before me, and I wash the back of his neck, bringing the suds up to his head. Latsil wears the sides and back of his head shaved but the top half is swept back into a short ponytail that almost looks like a man bun.

"Close your eyes," I whisper.

When he closes them, I use my fingernails to lovingly scrape soap gently along his forehead, down the sides of his face, across the bridge of his nose, under his chin, down his neck, and finally, when every inch of him is covered in fresh smelling lather, I say, "Hold your breath." And then I release the rope that triggers a water spray. He raises his face to allow the water to rinse down and all at once I'm caught by how beautiful this man is. Sharp cheekbones, a square jaw, and darker stubble lines defines his look, but his eyebrows and hair are slightly different than the usual orc shade. His hair is light brown, tinged with green. He raises himself to his full height, and then begins to wash me. His large hands are everywhere, kneading the top muscles of my shoulders, working the knots out of my back. Large thumbs massage the area down my spine and over my hips. I'm boneless, melting with desire when he even slips his fingers down my crack to wash me thoroughly between my buttocks.

He chuckles at my moans and when it's time to rinse off, we take another dousing under the bucket together. Finally, Latsil reaches for the robes hanging just outside our stall door. He covers me first, wrapping me securely in the fluffy thick cotton, and tying the belt around me. Only then does he put his own robe on, slow enough that the act is sultry, before lifting me and carrying me up the back way to our room.

Chapter Seven

*J**oanna:***

     We enter our room through the back patio doors. Latsil carefully places me on the bed, then spreads out his large body next to me.

"I'll be gentle, *cara'jek*," he says.

"I'm not worried." Because I can't help myself, I wrap my hand around his neck and bring his lips to mine. It's not the first time I've kissed him, but this is the first time I kiss him and show him what's in my heart.

Little quivers of excitement shoot down to my belly as our robes fall open and our bare skin touches. I can feel the hot, hard rod of his cock where it juts like an arm against my belly. I run my palm up his pecs... they're perfect and warm with a light smattering of hair.

His hungry gaze focuses on my breasts. A wicked smile touches his masculine lips, and his pupils constrict to pinpoints.

"For such a tiny thing, you're definitely well formed," he mutters.

"Are you thinking about how it might look to have the head of your cock buried between them, milord?"

"Gods," he grits.

I push the robe off his shoulders so he's utterly naked on the bed. Strong, fierce, scarred, tattooed, absolutely perfect.

Scooting down the bed, I bend his knees apart so I can fit between his legs. His abs flex as I run my hands up the muscles at his hips. His cock is hard as a rock, standing straight up, so I bend my head and lick.

I'm rewarded by the deepest, most guttural groan I've ever heard, and it makes me eager for more reaction from him. I take the thick head of his cock past my lips and circle him with my tongue as his hands go to my hair. He's trying to be gentle as he grips my head, but I can feel the power and strength in his hands.

I make a game of licking his cock, guiding him into my mouth, sucking deep, swirling my tongue around the head, licking lightly, sucking deep, and starting all over again.

He groans, his thigh muscles twitching as I grip the base of him harder and suck him in faster, as deep into my throat as I can, which is admittedly not very deep. I give him lots of licking, lots of kissing, because that's how Latsil likes it. He loves to be touched. And I love to touch him. He's an absolutely gorgeous specimen, dark and dangerous and yet sweet at the same time.

I can tell he's losing control by the tension in his legs. His face is strained as he stares down at me, taking in the image of my lips stretched around his cock. His entire body trembles; even his abs quiver.

"The sight of you... your gorgeous mouth sucking on my cock... I wish I could have an image of this permanently ingrained in my head."

I pop the head of his cock out of my mouth and lick it, swirling my tongue around it. "Well, whenever you start to forget, you just let me know and I'll get right down here again."

"You'll kill me," he says.

That's when I decide to show him what his cock looks like popping up from between my breasts. I squeeze my breasts around the wet, slick skin of him and when the head of his cock peers from where it's nestled in my cleavage, I bend my head and lick the massive beast.

With a groan, he hauls me up and presses a kiss to my mouth before he starts kissing down my body. The brute strength of him is magnificent. I can feel every powerful pull and he can easily overpower me with those huge muscles.

Yet I feel safer than I ever have. He's a brutal beast that wouldn't hurt a fly.

He licks every inch of me, from my neck to my toes, and even kisses the shell of my ear. It's like he's committing me to memory. The deep ache inside me won't stop until he fills me.

"Latsil, please," I beg, spreading my legs and trying to grip around his waist with my feet as I pull his arms up.

He stretches his entire length out over me.

When he poises before my entrance, he says, "You're soaked, but are you sure? Are you sure you want this? Because I may not be able to let you go afterward."

"Yes! Please, give it to me. I want you so bad."

Very slowly, as if determined I'll break, he slides into me. I use my feet to grip his ass and hold on, trying to get him so deep we can't tell where he ends, and I begin.

"So tight," he groans. "So wet. So ready for me."

"I've been ready forever. Now, start stroking."

He chuckles. "Greedy little minx."

But then he pulls out and thrusts back in and I feel every swollen inch of him slicing right through my slick body. He sets a rhythm and whispers into my ear how beautiful I am, how he was so lucky to have found me, how he knew right there in that diner that he wanted me even then but didn't think it would ever be possible. Not a human and an orc.

A whore and an orc, that's another story.

When our heartbeats thump faster and our breathing quickens and I can feel I'm at the edge, I lick his neck and beg him to thrust harder and faster.

By the time my body seizes with wonderful, clenching waves of climatic pleasure that pulse through every cell, he groans when my sheath clenches him tight with magnificent spasms and grits his teeth. He waits until my orgasm finishes before he pulls out and shoots his seed on my belly, then collapses, pulling me tightly against him, keeping the heated mess smeared between us.

"You have ten minutes to catch your breath, *cara'jek*, and then I will pleasure you with my tongue."

W e make love three more times before my stomach growls. We quickly clean up, sponge bathing each other, and I find a closet of sundresses that Latsil's bought for me. I swear he's the most caring male I've ever met. Three of the dresses are yellow, one is a bright golden color of a dandelion, one is the paler shade of butter, and the third is white and yellow patterned gingham.

"Yellow is your favorite color?" I ask.

"How did you guess?" he asks.

I slide the gingham over my head with a giggle. Should I find the merchant, I'll slip her a message for more yellow fabrics for me. It looks pretty good with my brown hair, bringing out golden highlights and making my skin look sun-kissed.

Right now, it's orc-kissed.

I smile shyly at him, angling my head up to see if he'll kiss me again. He groans and doesn't resist. I crave his kisses, the way his wider lips pucker between his tusks, the way his eyes glow like he can't believe I want to kiss him.

"If your stomach was not growling like an orc's, I'd take you again, sweet. But let's get you fed so you'll have strength, aye?"

I can't help the wide curve of my mouth as I admit to him, "I'm so happy."

"As am I," he whispers.

Hand in hand, we walk through the halls. At the diner of the inn, we find the others in his guard already seated. The ill-mannered brutes cheer like teenagers as we enter, and I can't help but flush and grin broadly. Latsil leads me to the table where they sit.

"If you had missed dinner, I was going to take your plates up to your room," Kreele says with a wink.

"It feels a little odd not to have Joanna cooking for us," Azorr says. "I enjoyed that stew you made."

"Chili," I say. "Usually, it's made with a side of cornbread. I'll have to show the cooks how to make it."

"You fit right into the clan perfectly," he compliments and I'm not sure if he knows how wonderful that makes me feel.

"So how is our whore taking to her training?" Kreele asks.

"She is not our whore," Latsil growls. "Joanna is off limits."

Brun's eyes twinkle. "Yes, she is in training for three moons. We remember."

Something makes me think they jest. Surely, they can all tell Latsil is the only one I want?

"'Tis all right." I caress the frown lines on Latsil's suddenly grumpy forehead. "I only have eyes for you."

Just like that, his face clears and the others cheer again, making me aware they teased him into his sullen mood to see what I'd do.

"I swear she's like a magic potion," Terk says, taking a bite of his bread. "Never have seen the brute grin so much. Looks ridiculous."

"Even when we play him," Azorr agrees.

Gorvan grunts.

"How long has your team been together?" I ask Latsil.

"Since we were dirty brats playing in the mud," he says. "We know all each other's secrets. Strengths and weaknesses."

I deliberately let my face fall. "Oh. Then you shall miss one or two if I poison his soup?"

He guffaws as the rest roar with laughter and Brun grabs a rather long breadstick to bop my fingers with. The bread breaks in half and he takes a bite of his half while I bite the other left on my plate.

"She really is perfect," Terk says, and his eyes connect with Latsil's.

While it could sound as if he might be interested in me as a whore for all, I don't think he means it that way. Not after all the males know of Latsil's possessive streak. Still, I feel Latsil bristle, and I wonder why he's so jealous when the truth is, I am but a whore.

Chapter Eight

Joanna:

As soon as we get back to Solaya, Latsil and the others work on the construction of my cabin. He'd surprised me on the way home by showing me the contents of the half-carriage we were carting home. Packed carefully with padding between them were real glass windows. A large one with two slender ones to be placed side by side of the larger, all on the sewing wall. He'll build shutters so I can shut out the sun when it gets too warm. Then he shows me a bigger surprise... a sewing machine, one where I use my foot to tap a pedal and make the needle bob up and down while I steer the edge of the fabric underneath. He's thought of everything.

And I thank him. Over and over again, with my lips, and my tongue, and my body rocking over his, under his. With our pleasured cries, which I try to muffle when we're in his tent.

During one of our many nights when we lay in his furs, I'd told him I was a farmer's daughter, and that I'm surprised the orcs don't grow their own food. Instead, they take the time to purchase vegetables at markets hours away, though they find and use wild onions and dandelions. It makes more sense when he tells me they're not completely familiar with growing our foods. When the portal had opened merging our worlds, several orc clans had fallen through before it snapped shut. On our side, Earth lost whole cities. It was long, long ago and the entire world was rerouted, remapped with a new way of thinking. What little technology we had was considered to have begun the whole downfall, for it was our technology that opened the portal to another world.

Today he's putting the finishing touches on my cabin, including a raised garden where I can grow my own crop. I know he intends to keep me well fed and taken care of, but this is my chance to teach his people how to be more self-sufficient also. I'm not sure where they mine their gold, but surely it can't last forever, and I'm not a farmer's daughter for nothing. While my father's farm may be gone, his knowledge continues on. Perhaps his farm might live on one day in the village of the orcs. It will all begin with my garden.

I wait for the sound of construction to begin before I sneak out of his tent. It's a little hard to stay inconspicuous in one of my new sundresses. It's bright yellow, but Latsil loves it, and I can't wait for him to see me in it later.

This is finally the right moment to head toward Vinshesa's. I've been dying to confront her, but she's never alone. The perfect moment arose when Vin was bleary eyed from ale last night and headed inside early. I watched her, knowing she'd sleep late, and knowing as soon as Latsil left in the morn, I intended to race over and give her a piece of my mind. I've been waiting for this chance since we returned from the trip to Creede, and I learned she'd been mated to him. Though, I'm not sure what upsets me more, that she was mated to my man or that she killed his first mate. I should be madder about the latter, but I must confess to jealousy, and it's ugly inside me.

"Vin! Vin! Get up, you lazy tramp!" I shout, lifting the flap to her tent and closing it behind me. It's dark inside but I can make out the lump of her beneath the blankets.

"I swear I'll douse you with water if you don't get out of bed this instant," I snarl, yanking the blankets off the bed in one fell swoop.

Sleepy protests follow my rage—protests, as in two. A male voice and hers.

I stare stunned into silence at two different shades of green bodies on the bed, not one.

Kreele's naked ass stares me in the face.

"Did you forget the lesson that says a whore's home is sacred?" Vinshesa asks. "To treat her home with honor and respect?"

I ignore her question and scratch my head, my anger temporarily forgotten. "I'm more confused by the one that says whores tend to males in their—the male's—quarters."

First it was Terk ensconced in Bessica's furs, now it's Bess's brother in Vinshesa's. It makes me wonder who Grunalda is sneaking around with and whether or not she knows of the secret lovers of these two.

"I'm going to guess that no one knows about this," I say, motioning to the two bodies.

"Of course not," Vinshesa says as she narrows her eyes at me. "And we'll keep it that way."

"I seem to be a vessel for secrets," I snap, rolling my eyes that they think they'll need to zip my lips.

"Oh? Do tell," Vin taunts.

"Absolutely not." I glare at her for even suggesting such a thing.

"*M'kirn*, please? It's chilly." Kreele yawns and points at his bared ass.

Flushing, I scatter the blankets back on top of them and since there's such a wide expanse of bed unused, I crawl up onto that side, kicking off my slippers and poking my toes under the warm blanket.

"I won't tell on one condition," I bluster. "That you tell me the whole story of why you killed Latsil's mate. Why you mated him just to leave him because that's what it sounds like. And"—I take a deep breath— "why you never told me you were mated to him. I thought we were friends!"

"Aye, we're friends," she says softly.

Then there's complete silence from the two orcs cuddled together in the bed, but the blanket moves and Vin flashes me a view of her hand curled around Kreele's huge green dick.

I slide my feet out and away.

Kreele's voice is mild when he answers. "Seems to me you're a good secret keeper already, aren't you, *m'kirn*? So, there's not really any bargaining power here."

I sigh. "Well, yes."

Vinshesa chuckles. Kreele slips out of bed, stands, and stretches. Again, I avert my eyes from his dangling member.

He kisses Vin before he starts to dress. "I'll leave you two to sort out your secrets," he says.

We wait until he's fully dressed, then watch as he peers outside the tent flap to make sure no one is around before he slips out. Then Vinshesa sits up in bed, propping herself on the pillow next to me, though she's still naked as the day she was born.

I deliberately focus straight up at the ceiling as I grab the blanket and tuck it around her boobies. She sighs but allows it and then we sit back and stare at the canvas ceiling.

The mood grows somber as she thinks back.

"The truth is, none of us could stand what was going on. Tavri was from one of the southern clans and her ways were very different than ours. But Latsil fell for her hard, and with no one around to decide whether or not it was a good idea, he mated her. Bess, Grun, and I suspected that she wanted his status. After some research, we learned that in their clan a mate was entitled to all, even after the loss of her male. And after all, Latsil is the right-hand guard for Brun. He was wealthy and"—her voice drops to a whisper— "he used to be handsome. The largest, most skilled brute we had. Kind and generous, and fair."

"He's still handsome!" I interject, turning to scowl at her. She's still staring at the top of the tent.

She absently pats my hand.

"One day, Latsil disappeared. We searched everywhere, for many moons, and we questioned everyone for his whereabouts, especially Tavri. Oh, how she cried and carried on for her lost love. But we three weren't fooled, despite everyone else comforting her like she was the victim."

"*Hyiak*, ho," a voice calls outside the tent flap.

"Inside," Vinshesa snaps, irritated that she's being interrupted. "Hurry up. I'm telling pipsqueak the story of when Lats disappeared."

Grunalda and Bessica enter, carrying a small tub of steaming water between them.

"We saw Kreele on his way to go work on Jo-Jo's cabin," Bess says as they set the tub down. "He said you called out for this earlier and didn't know if anyone was around to bring it since they're all out there."

Poor innocent Bessica.

I roll my eyes when she's looking down. Vinshesa nudges me with her elbow, which makes me giggle. Bessica is absolutely clueless that her brother is sleeping with her best friend.

"I heard you had a hard night," Bess says quietly to Vinshesa as she comes to join us on the bed.

Vinshesa looks down. And for the first time, I see the bags under her eyes. I can't help but feel bad that I caused her more worry than just being discovered with Bessica's brother. I slip my hand into hers, silently promising her I'll keep my word. And she curls my smaller fingers against hers.

But then I remember the same hand was curled on Kreele's dick and my fingers stretch out and stiffen.

She chuckles as if she knows what I'm thinking, and then lets go of my hand to hook her arm around my neck, pulling me to her. I catch a whiff of their combined scent and have to fight against wrinkling my nose.

Bessica doesn't notice. Grunalda, on the other hand, studies me carefully.

Still chuckling, Vin deposits a hard kiss on top of my head before she slips out of the bed and heads to the small bathing tub. I look away when she squats over it to wash her lady bits. She has no grace.

"Then you all knew about it?" I ask her. "You all felt uneasy about Tavri?"

"Aye. The entire clan was uneasy around her. Latsil was never given permission by Brachard to bring her into Mont Grove. Solaya was the furthest he could bring her, and he still didn't see the red flags," Vinshesa says.

"And one day, he freed himself from his capture. We found him halfway home, having dragged himself from the Blackheart Village. We declared war and lost many orcs in the battle on their side. We only relented when their leader offered a tentative truce with ours," Bessica says.

Grunalda cuts in. "He said one person from our side gave him information of where Latsil would be on that day, that he would be alone and unprotected in the river awaiting his mate. You see, only Latsil knew that Tavri was going to meet him for a picnic near the river. He was to bathe first and be ready for her by the time she arrived. But she never did. And she conveniently never told a soul about this rendezvous. When confronted, she said it was something private between her and Latsil. And she simply didn't want to embarrass him by everyone knowing he was dragged off naked and weaponless, a huge disgrace. She found his clothes later and took them home. It was obvious she was covering it up. But Latsil still believed her," Vinshesa says.

"That's when we knew we had to take matters into our own hands. The males would never do so. And the king had no jurisdiction over Latsil. We had watched Latsil's self-confidence drop with every ugly word Tavri uttered. Things grew even more tense when she whined that he needed to work on a way to get them to live in the mountain. He was a shell of a man, torn between protecting the female he loved from the family he loved."

"Now, because of this whole situation, the king has jurisdiction over all the royal guard who no longer have elders," Bessica says sadly. "A lesson learned too late."

"So... was all of this a set up?" I ask all three of them. "You're trying to get Latsil over his horrible relationship by using me?"

"No, it's not like that," Bess says. "He was a changed man after her death. Never smiled again. But you, Jo-Jo. You bring out the best in him from the first day he met you. Everyone says so."

"Do you think I didn't notice how angry Latsil became when I suggested you become a whore? He couldn't stand the thought of others with you," Vinshesa says. "These two saw it too, but I made sure to suggest it because he is already angry with me and that will never go away. But I also knew that making you a whore was the only way he would feel safe with you. A whore doesn't mate, and Latsil will never feel safe enough to mate again. So, I gave you both the perfect solution."

"Until it's time for me to take others."

"We'll deal with that when it comes," Bessica says, waving her hand as if it's not important. "You're one of us. We'll take care of you."

"Besides," Grunalda says. "I'm sure the males of his crew know how he feels about you. Kreele, Terk, Azorr. None of them will touch you."

"Lats thinks Terk is interested in me," I mention. "He caught us walking together, one morn. As we left your tent."

"And you couldn't say why you were walking with Terk?" Grunalda says thoughtfully. "Pipsqueak is definitely one of us. Way to take one for the team," she says, raising her hand to slap mine open-palmed. And I know I'm not imagining the awareness in her eyes.

"Latsil told Kreele that Tavri couldn't bear his scars. That they horrified her and reminded her of the violence of war. His health deteriorated without the love of his mate. Tavri became angry and bitter because Latsil, our lost soul, returned and all our attention was on him. She was no longer the sobbing widow. Now she was back to her previously established status where she couldn't even visit Mont Grove.

She'd really banked on being able to stay in the underground kingdom," Vin says as she starts dressing.

"She began to call him names. Brute. Ugly. Animal. She would wake in the middle of the night and pretend to be so frightened by his appearance, he'd have to go outside to sleep. The other males were frustrated, but Latsil would hear nothing negative about his mate, including the theory that she was the one who gave the information to the Blackhearts. He became bitter. And mistrusting of others in the village as he wondered who might have betrayed him," Grunalda says.

Bessica leans in, her eyes flashing. "And then Tavri focused her attentions on my brother. Naturally, Latsil was jealous. Latsil and Kreele began to fight. One night while they were out brawling, I gave Tavri a beating, later blaming it over a night of too much ale. It felt so good at the time, but Latsil accused me of doing it purposely. Kreele jumped to my defense, and it made already tense relations between the two males even worse. Terk stepped in, but Latsil accused him of taking sides, of having a crush on a favored whore. It's why we keep under wraps today. Things were going from bad to worse."

"Our last option was to petition the king," Vin says. She looks haunted.

"There were no other choices left." Bessica cuts in with a scowl as if she doesn't want Vinshesa to blame herself. "King Brachard was at the point where he had to make a decision regarding the brawling males. Brun couldn't be fully protected with guards who warred among each other. The king was down to two options; he could banish Latsil or he could remove his title of first guard, which might be even worse because then Terk or Kreele would take his place. Talk about rubbing salt in an open wound."

"So, I asked Brachard if Latsil's line might end with their lack of whelps instead of living on within our clan. That he was one of the largest males, and the fastest. The best trained. And that I was ready to have brats. We all knew that Tavri wasn't. She made it clear that Latsil, with all his new scars, was no longer to touch her. We used that against her and petitioned the king to allow me to also mate Latsil. You see, the king has jurisdiction over the whores. And now with Latsil's downfall, he had jurisdiction over Lats. So, I was introduced. Naturally, Tavri wouldn't allow us to have a wedding night. She claimed petty jealousy. And for the first time ever, allowed Latsil to cuddle her through her fits. I could see the hope in his eyes that perhaps she might grow used to his scars. And I knew it was but another game with her. I did not insist on my marriage night. Because that's not why I was in the mating. Instead, I waited until he left on a trip, happier than he'd ever been from her newfound attention. And I killed her."

A chill rolls up my spine. Her words are so nonchalant. Yet there's a somber feeling in the tent as the other two relive the story.

"We three knew Vinshesa's punishment would be banishment from her new mating, along with banishment from future matings. She'll never be eligible for another," Bessica says. "A whore ever more." She places her hand over Vin's.

"A whore ever more," Grunalda repeats and puts her hand over Bessica's.

That's why the three of them are determined to remain whores. They know that Vinshesa will always be one, and they made a pact to remain single forever. That's why Bessica keeps her relationship with Terk under wraps.

"That didn't go over well for him," I explain softly. "He'd hoped to have another mate's support while he grieved his true love, but you were gone too."

Vinshesa winces. "We couldn't allow that. Much as I love him, I couldn't let him transfer false feelings to me. That would be wrong."

Huh.

Chapter Nine

Latsil:

Kreele sweeps the last of the dust from the wooden floors. Outside, Terk, Ogol, and Brun fill the dirt into the raised boxes, while Azorr is polishing the windows. Gorvan is planting bushes as a wind block along the side of the house.

Everything is perfect for her.

"*Hyiak*," Beth calls out from the doorway.

I grunt in reply, heading her way.

Her eyes twinkle as she speaks. "Terk has gone to let them know to bring her in. I'm sure the two of you will want to break in that new bed," she angles her head toward the bed area, "so I'm just going to leave this with you." She holds out a small satchel filled with small bottles, human writing on each one. "Seeds. I picked them up in Creede before we left. A bit of everything, she can plant whatever she wants. And tell her whenever I'm here, I'll help with weeding and stuff."

A smile breaks out over my face. I had planned to take her for some herself since I had no idea what it was she would want or need, but this is perfect.

Beth is staring at me like I grew an extra set of tusks. Has it really been that long since I smiled? Or does smiling pull on my scars horrifically and frighten her? I turn away, but I'm surprised when she places her hand on my bicep.

"I really like Joanna," she says simply, and then turns and leaves.

I head inside to place the gift on the table, and then go back outside to wait.

Down the path I see Terk leading three females—and then there is my lovely Joanna, dressed in my favorite color. Yellow. The bright shade of the sun.

My heart stops when I take in her beauty.

"Hi, Lats," she whispers shyly. "Is this my cabin? It's lovely."

"Not as lovely as you, *m'kirn*," I say gallantly, recovering use of my tongue and ignoring Terk's snort at my effort. "May I show you inside?"

She places her small hand in mine, and I can't help but beam. I lead her indoors and show her the table first, ignoring the other four loud-mouths behind us. "That is a housewarming gift from Beth. Seeds. She says plant whatever you want and when she is in the village, she'll help you weed and care for them."

"Oh, she's so sweet!" Joanna says.

"What?" Vinshesa says, scowling. "As your best friends, we were going to help you too, Jo-Jo. On cooler days, because Grunalda doesn't like to sweat."

"Agreed," Grunalda says with a shudder.

"Thanks, ladies," Joanna says, perfectly sweet as if we're not all aware the lazy whores won't complain about digging in dirt when the opportunity arises.

The three beam at her like I haven't seen in years, as if they love making Joanna happy.

Happy. That's what Joanna brings to our village. She has our squabbling orcs—who all got along until I mated—getting along easier, the way we used to before petty jealousy tore us all apart.

"Oh, that bed is beautiful!" Joanna exclaims, fingering the wooden frame I handcrafted.

Terk slaps his hand on my shoulder. "Latsil is good with wood."

Grunalda snickers and I roll my eyes. Best if I take her away from the fools. "Come, *cara'jek*, let me show you the gardens," I growl, taking her out the back door and wondering why I see the eyes on the orcs widen. Oh... I referred to her as my sweetheart instead of a maiden in front of them.

But I don't care what they think.

"Latsil! You did all this for me?" Her voice is overcome with emotion before Joanna bursts into tears.

"Joanna?" I ask, baffled as I hold her to my chest.

"You're so good to me," she sobs. "I swear, you're the best orc in the whole village."

"I'm not one for tears," Vinshesa says. "What say we all go get some grub?"

The others grumble a reply and the four of them leave.

"The details of your home, *cara'jek*," I say softly, wishing to distract her from her tears. "I built your cabin on an incline, see? With wooden walk paths. You can sit on the porch if you like. Or you can sit in your garden. When I return from the trip to Serenity, I will build you an overhang for shade."

I'm not sure why I'm babbling on so frantically other than I want to make sure this female understands Solaya is a safe place for her. That she'll be happy here... with me. I steer her back indoors.

"And you are on the edge of the village near the creek. We have a pump for water, see? If there is not enough rain, it can be pumped for your gardens. Too much rain, and your cabin will be safe because of the incline it was built on. And the wooden walks? I added sand to the wood preservative so it would not get so slippery when wet."

She holds her fingers up to my lips to stop my incessant babbling.

"I love what you've done for me, Lats. It's perfect. No one has ever done so much."

What? I've barely done anything for this incredible creature. How can no one do what she considers so much?

"I'd just like to ask one more thing of you."

Cold fingers grip my insides in icy clutches. I've been through this before. A sudden image of Tavri comes to mind, begging, pleading for one more thing. One last thing that I cannot give her... access to the underground living at Mont Grove. I could never go against our king, who didn't trust an orc from the southern clan, despite the fact she was my mate.

Joanna looks up at me with her gray eyes and perfectly pink lips.

"What is it you wish, *cara'jek*?" I ask, my voice thick, dreading her answer but knowing I will do anything to give her what she wants.

"Will you christen my home with me, Lats?" she purrs.

And those icy tendrils disappear as I realize what she's getting at.

I grab her hand and haul her to the back walk. She giggles behind me as I bellow outside to the orcs wandering in her gardens, "Everybody out!"

I slam the door on the shocked faces, show Joanna how the inside shutters work on her floor-length windows, and when the house is dark and closed from nosy orc eyes, we christen her new bed.

J *oanna:*

Latsil has become a lust-crazed beast. He drops me onto the bed and kisses me the entire time he peels the clothing from my body, leaving me naked while he's still dressed. It feels naughty like this and heat blooms in my pussy as he kisses me over and over.

More heat blooms when I think he may kiss my pussy.

I can tell he wants to as his hands stroke over me, as he plays with my nipple between his teeth, when he sucks the tip of my breast into his mouth so deeply, I have a mini release while my legs are spread wide, and my open sex is untouched.

"Good girl," he growls, and his eyes have a dangerous glint. Dominant, arrogant, and determined to please me. "Now bent your legs at the knees and draw them up. I wish for your pussy to open naturally for me."

I do as he asks, feeling carnal and full of sin as I hold my legs wide. He settles between them on the bed. "That's the prettiest pussy I've ever seen."

Ooh, this orc makes me feel pretty, indeed.

Latsil slides his hands up my thighs. "I can see the slickness between the puffy lips of your cunt, *cara'jek*. You want this, don't you? A brutal orc sucking your cunt?"

I shiver involuntarily, my pulse thundering in my ears. There's no way to lie. "Yes."

"I want to eat this pussy every night. I want to feel you come on my tongue, with my fingers deep inside you while you beg for my cock."

When his mouth touches me, I cry out at the sensation of instant heat. His tongue drags ruthlessly across my swollen flesh, lapping at the juices he finds, licking at the sensitive pearl that peeks from my folds, wanting his attention. He growls, spreading me open to spear his tongue inside, toying with my clit by licking it rhythmically, then delving deep into my center and back again. He's hunched over, his massive shoulders rounded, and the sound of him eating my pussy is sloppy and wet. I love it.

I love being his whore.

He raises his head, and his eyes are dilated, taking in the sight of my flushed face, my heaving breasts with the beaded nipples poking stiffly with arousal.

"Such a pretty little thing, giving yourself so completely to me," he growls.

"Yes," I say. "Take what you need. Give me what I need in return."

SAVED BY THE ORC77

"You need an orc, sweet."

Not just any orc, but I keep my words to myself.

He dives back in, and I start shuddering under the onslaught. His mouth wreaks havoc on the tender flesh of my pussy and my orgasm sneaks up on me, making me shriek out with pleasure. He watches me climax, his hands cupping my swollen breasts as I come down from my sudden high.

"I've never seen such a beautiful sight," he grits.

"Do you think you might make me come again?" I ask, my voice still quivering along with the rest of my limbs. "This time with your beautiful cock stroking inside me? Coaxing another orgasm from me?"

"Joanna." He shuts his eyes, his face wrenched in pain as if he can't believe I would want his cock.

"Fill me up, Latsil," I purr. "Stroke it deep inside, over and over until I come again, squeezing and milking you with my climax. Only then are you allowed to come, you hear? You'll be allowed to pull out and come on my belly. On my pussy. Or on my nipples. Splash wherever you want."

He nods, bemused by my words.

I smile sultrily, knowing there's no way this orc can control his need long enough to shoot come on top of me, not with my pussy squeezing him so tight.

He presses his thick, meaty pole inside me slowly, closing his eyes, pleasure strewn all over his face. He thrusts just a little more each time, going a bit deeper slowly, but I want it all. I'm having a difficult time re-straining myself as I wrap my legs around his waist and try to pull him deeper into me. He holds himself in a pushup position so the only parts of us touching are my pussy and his cock, and it feels like he's slicing through butter, hot, wet, and slick.

Finally, he's balls deep. From the tight clench of his jaw, he can bare-ly restrain himself, and reaches down to press his thumb on my clit.

Pleasure zings from the spot, more so when he circles it. He wants me to come because he can't keep from losing his seed.

I love this. I love having this much power over such a strong male.

My blood is pumping hot through my veins.

"Fuck me deeply, milord. Make me come, and then you may. I shall lick your cock clean for you, and then you can go again."

I smile when he snarls at my filthy words and send a thanks up to the three whores who taught me how to talk dirty to a male.

His stroking changes to long and deep, returning the control to him, and I can't contain myself as I come again, his cock, hard as a rock, sluicing through my pussy even though the grip is so tight as I clench around him, my shuddery climax going on and on.

"Fuck, Joanna," he grits, and I think I feel a splash of liquid inside me before he pulls out, come frantically spewing in spurts from the tip of his cock. He smears it over my clit, and the hot seed runs in rivulets down my slit. He pumps himself as he continues to come, splashing on my belly as he groans and seals his mouth to mine.

"Gods, you're perfect," he says, between kisses. "So utterly perfect."

Chapter Ten

J*oanna:*

Before I know it two months go by and I'm more than halfway through my whore training. I have a dilemma because I need to know how to gently turn down other males, but the three gals haven't told me a thing about turning down anyone.

Grunalda looked at me like I was crazy and asked why I wouldn't want to sleep with someone new. Bessica shrugged and said she'd never done it. Vinshesa grunted and then mumbled that I'd figure it out.

What happened to banding together? I'd stomped off in a fit, ignoring their tusk-y grins.

Despite the problem of what to do now that I'm a soon-to-be full-fledged whore, I have everything I've always wanted.

Imagine my surprise when Brun's new bride is none other than Lady Hannah Montierge of Serenity, my childhood fantasy friend. It was scandalous too, turns out Brun knew her when they were children, though Hannah had fevers and can no longer remember. And when her father arranged the marriage, she'd refused and was held overnight in his jail. The guards there branded her back. The scarring should disqualify her from remaining an orcen princess. If she does get to stay, this is my chance to have everything I ever wanted... my man, my own house, and now my best friend.

Not that she knows we're best friends yet.

I've tried a hundred times to talk to her and failed miserably, despite the three gals trying to help out. They came up with a great plan of giving her a new dress, custom-designed by me, even name dropped me to her, saying I was the best human dressmaker in the village. Which, technically, being the only dressmaker, I am.

I've talked to Latsil about wanting to be friends with Hannah. He assures me she's nice and it's only natural for us to fall into our best friend status, since he is with Brun. I promised to take the plunge and visit her sometime today. Maybe after I watch his training.

Maybe after lunch.

Maybe before it grows dark.

I feel like a stalker as I wait for her to come out of her tent this morn. Hopefully she won't be too long because I'd like to watch Latsil train.

I just can't do it. I turn to leave, but then her tent flap opens and she's here, right in my path, and she'll notice me scuttling away like a cockroach.

"H-Hannah? I'm Joanna." I wait nervously for her reaction. Surely her eyes will glaze over, and she'll politely walk away.

"Joanna! Oh, my gosh, I've been meaning to thank you for my lovely gown."

Just like that, all my insecurities drop away. She liked the gown I lovingly stitched for her. "Oh, it's nothing. I used to sew... before. When I lived in Granby. Anyway, I heard about them slicing it to see the brand on your back. I thought I could probably fix it for you."

"You can? Oh, I could never ask that—"

"It'll be easy enough. I can cut it into a V, hem the edges, and lace it together. In fact, if you want, I can use the lacings to frame your brand. You can wear your hair down to cover it, but it'll be easy to lift and move aside should someone wish to see your mark without having to ruin your clothes."

"That would have been much easier," she says, smiling with me and nodding. She gestures for me to follow her inside her tent.

I stand awkwardly while she rummages through the wooden wardrobe she shares with Brun. Then she spreads it out on the bed. I lean over it, studying the edges that were sliced with a sword.

"Yes, I think the lacing would be a better choice. And sexier." I can't help but wink. "Your orc will appreciate it."

"Thank you," she says, her cheeks pink.

All at once I'm alarmed. Was that too forward of me? She is a lady, things are not spoken so openly with the higher class, though in my head I was thinking we already had a closer relationship between us. I could kick myself for my foolishness.

I pick up the gown and fold it over my arm. My insecurities rear their ugly head again as we run out of things to say.

"Where were you headed when I so rudely stopped you?" I ask suddenly, feeling my cheeks heat. She's so well-mannered and I'm so rude.

"I was just, uh, looking for Brun."

"He's sparring," I say, wanting to be helpful. Would she possibly want company? "I wanted to go watch too. Do you want to go together?" I'm terrified she'll turn me down. She should turn me down, she's royalty and I'm nothing but a farmer's daughter.

Hannah studies me carefully.

"I'd like that," she says, and she smiles. It's so beautiful and freeing and for the first time, I feel like we are on similar levels. Maybe we both need this friendship.

"Okay." I agree happily. "We'll drop off your dress at my place on the way."

Hannah follows me as we head down the winding trails.

"How did you know he was sparring?" she asks.

"Oh, I go to watch every morning. Latsil will be there."

"Latsil?"

"He's... he's my favorite," I whisper. Sometimes it feels too good to be true.

My cabin comes into sight. "See this little cabin? It's mine. He built it for me."

I hold open the door for her, hoping she'll find it as adorable as I do.

"Wow, he built this for you?" she asks, openly studying my home.

"He says he always wants me to have a place where I can be safe. And he's right. Since he built it last summer, I've only been to trading villages twice. I picked up all the fabric I needed and spend most of my time here."

"You have enough to eat?"

Just like a best friend, she's worried about me—a single woman—living here. "I trade vegetables from my garden in the summer to anyone who wants some. Orcs aren't used to farming; they're used to living off the land. But in the winter, they're so appreciative they drop off meat at my doorstep." Not to mention, Latsil would never let me starve. I lay her dress over my sewing table and point to the back door. "May as well head out that way. We'll be walking around the house anyway." And actually, I'd like to show off my garden, though I don't mention it.

She doesn't disappoint. She blinks as we walk through the raised garden maze and then raises her eyebrow as if to ask me how I own such an amazing work of art.

"Latsil again. He didn't like me bending over."

She grins.

We make our way back down to the edge of the village.

"How do you know Bessica, Grunalda, and Vinshesa?" she asks.

"They've been my friends for a long time. Bess is the one who told me exactly how to please Latsil when I arrived. She noticed his gaze on me a lot and knew he was intrigued."

The sounds of grunting and cheering ring out as we draw closer. "They've got a crowd today," I say. "Probably since the king and queen are here."

King Brachard and his queen, Aga, arrived to meet Brun's new wife. It didn't go great, they'd been upset that she was branded and had sliced her gown—the one I'm going to fix—from her back to see the scar.

Most everyone is sitting closer to the arena, but we choose to sit on bales of hay on the outskirts of the crowds to watch. I made the suggestion after Hannah paused slightly when seeing all the spectators gathered up front, and figured since she was a newcomer, she was probably nervous. She looked so grateful, plus I was glad to have her to myself for just a little longer, so we sat down further away. I try to explain as much as I can to her since this is her first time watching, and we're huddled together, talking like real friends. I'd just explained to her that the guards' job is to protect Brun at all costs... until Hannah screams when Brun takes a dagger to the shoulder.

I lean forward immediately, tension filling my limbs. That can't be good. Orc guards will be punished if royalty is scarred, even by accident.

I follow her when she runs to him, and then everyone is running to where he's fallen. He seems fine enough, though the dagger sticks through him still.

King Brachard declares Ogol's life forfeited, who was the one who had landed the blow that is sure to scar. It's an odd rule, the orcs are tasked with training Brun to fight, yet punished if one scars his body.

And when the knife is pulled from Brun's shoulder, blood shoots out in geysers. His face pales and he leans back, looking at Hannah as his eyes go sightless.

I can't believe what I'm seeing, and I don't think anyone else can believe it either.

I move to comfort Hannah but then she goes into a sort of trance. The world slows down, the air thickens and then Latsil is there, his strong arms around me in his time of need, because Brun is his best friend.

I've never held him so tight. Hot tears flood my cheeks when a wave of incredulity passes over the crowd. Aga, Brun's mother, gasps. I push away from Latsil to see what's going on.

Brun is awake suddenly and talking to Hannah. Like a witch, she's drawn his soul back from death.

I'm not sure what miracle has happened, but Brun rises, the horrible wound in his shoulder that gushed blood like a river completely gone. He hugs and kisses his parents and then reaches for Latsil, his best friend. The two males hug and kiss each other's cheeks, tears streaming openly down their faces as they console each other.

I hug Hannah and we watch as, one by one, the other guards on his team touch foreheads with him.

Then Brun is hauling Hannah up into his arms and they head to his tent. Aga is still sobbing in Brachard's arms when Latsil goes silent.

I still can't believe what I think I saw. Surely Brun was dead? But no one is talking about it, instead people are still crying and whispering about lost orc magic, while others stand around in shock.

Then Latsil clears his throat. "I will go hunt for something special for dinner. Surely this is an evening for celebration?"

When King Brachard nods his head up and down, still unable to speak, Latsil turns on his heel and leaves.

Without a second glance at me.

"Latsil?" I call out, unsure what's going on.

He freezes on the path. "Joanna. I'm sure you can make your way to your cabin." He continues down the path without even looking back at me.

But Kreele stares thoughtfully at his retreating back and says gently, "Come, sweet. I will take you home."

And while Latsil avoided looking at me twice, I can't help but feel his eyes on me as Kreele escorts me, though that's probably wishful thinking.

"What just happened?" I ask Kreele as we get to my front porch.

"I think we all need personal time to ponder that question," Kreele responds carefully. "Spend some time relaxing. Sew, or putter in your garden. I imagine most of the village will be quiet today until the feast begins tonight. Do you want me to come back for you?"

"Nay, there is no need," I say, and muster as much dignity as I can, even though my heart is shattered. "I can make my way."

It's not my imagination that he looks relieved and then I realize that while he tells me to take personal time alone, he will spend his personal time with the one he loves. He'll visit Vinshesa while everyone is distracted. He's probably worried to death over her.

And that just makes me more despondent because that's where Lats and I should be. Consoling each other in our time of need. I'm so puzzled by his rejection.

"I will see you later tonight, then," Kreele says.

"Mmm. Thank you for walking me home, Kreele."

"Anytime, *m'kirn*." He bows, then leaves me at my front door.

Even though I know Latsil won't come, I can't help but wait for him. Which is ridiculous, because I heard, along with everyone else, that he would be hunting for tonight's celebration.

I work on making several salads for the feast. I have potatoes and tomatoes, mint, parsley, and chives. Cucumbers and zucchini. Lavender for drinks. Some carrot curls will make lovely decorations. I strip my garden, then take the huge basket to the main kitchen where several orcs are already preparing tonight's feast. I immerse myself in work, showing the others my bounty as we talk about the best ways to prepare what I've brought.

And finally, when the eve rolls around, when the meat is roasting and orcs begin to fill the yard, do I notice Latsil has returned.

Not once did he come by to see me. Something is very, very wrong.

"Jo-Jo, come," Grunalda calls out. "Saved you a spot."

Normally, the three are cuddled up to males somewhere, but this time they take their spots among the King's table. My cheeks burn as I realize everyone is aware something's up with Lats and me.

Grunalda's frown is fierce as she pulls me between her and Bessica. Bessica pulls the plate they've loaded toward me, even grabs the fork to place in my hand. For a moment I think she's going to start feeding me.

But then everyone settles down and we begin to eat.

At the opposite end of the table sit Brachard and Aga, with Brun and Hannah on their right. Latsil sits next to Hannah, followed by Kreele, Terk, and the rest of their guard on the opposite side of the queen.

"So, Joanna. You grew these vegetables?" Brachard booms down the table. "You've been quite an asset to our clan."

"Y-yes," I stutter, then cringe. I don't mean I'm an asset, I'm answering the first question, but his eyes aren't on me. They're on Latsil who is calmly eating his food as if there's no conversation taking place.

"You came to Solaya by yourself, yes?" Brachard asks.

"Yes, sir."

"Then you shall visit Mont Grove," he barks and slaps his hand on his thigh like there's no other discussion about it. "You shall see how the home front looks. All the orcs in Solaya visit back and forth."

I freeze. By the way everyone behaves, this is a big deal and I'm not sure how to respond. I can't look toward Hannah; she's too busy snuggling with Brun. And Lats is looking down, as if he angles his scars away from their king.

The king stares at him thoughtfully. "First Guard Latsil will bring you," Brachard says.

Through it all, the other guys—Brun, Kreele, Terk, Azorr, Gorvan—are all steadily quiet. I'm mortified. The tension in the room has never been so thick.

Chapter Eleven

L *atsil:*

For so long, I begged Brachard for permission to bring Tavri to the underground caves. It was always steadfastly denied. Yet in one fell swoop, the king has fallen under Joanna's spell just like every other orc in the village and he utters an invitation without reservation.

No one but me ever trusted Tavri. How had I not seen that until now? And if I was that wrong about her, what else was I wrong about? After Brun's death and immediate resurrection, I needed to get away. All I could think about was what if it had been me who'd issued the killing blow? The order for my death would have been immediate, and Joanna would have had to watch my execution and then spend the remainder of her days alone in an orc village I'd brought her to.

I'd give her Pegasus, of course. And all my funds and possessions, but they won't last the rest of her life. Mayhap I'm doing her more harm than good by being such a greedy male sucking up all her attentions. And now? Knowing that I've never made good decisions, I can't subject her to such a lacking fool as me. No, Joanna needs to go back to the humans where she can find a reasonable human man of her choosing, one who will worship her and give her the fruitful life that she deserves. Not waste her time on an ugly broken orc who can't even make quality decisions. An orc so easily swayed by a pretty face that he put his entire village at risk.

My heart freezes midbeat. What if Tavri had bargained with the Blackhearts to invade the village? I am lucky that she just bargained for my capture. And for the first time, I fully acknowledge that is what happened. The orcs didn't stumble upon me bathing in the river.

I distinctly remember Tavri telling me she would come sneak up on me and didn't want any of those "vile weapons" marring my "beautiful body." Aye, back then before the capture, I'd been a handsome male. More fool me, to fall for her trickery in letting me know in no uncertain terms to leave my weapons with my clothing on the bank. It was not so long ago that I stumbled upon Brun and his mate Hannah swimming in the creek. I brought them a blanket to dry off with, noticing even then that Brun wasn't unprotected. He still had his dagger strapped to his thigh. I am the only idiot who did everything my mate asked, including leaving myself completely defenseless and exposed. Taking Bessica to task for slapping Tavri when Bessica could stand her drama no longer. Resenting Kreele for stepping in to defend his sister, saying she only had my best interests at heart. Resenting Terk for stepping in to settle things when Kreele and I fought. And then accusing Terk of favoring Bessica simply because I knew it would cause issues between Terk and Kreele.

Deep shame fills me over that. Bessica had looked so betrayed, like I'd slapped her. And of course, Kreele ate it up, immediately jumping on Terk, who had been nothing but a friend to him. To both of us.

Not many know that all three whores were also downgraded when Vinshesa was banished from our mating. Brachard suspected it was all of them working together, but it couldn't be proven, not with Vinshesa taking all the blame for Grunalda and Bessica, so he hit them where it hurt. They were whores who could no longer accept coin. Though he never said so, Brun's way of fixing their demotion was to make them maids attending his new bride and offer them a small bit of wage. And while the three could have whined and thrown fits, much like my spoiled mate, instead they embraced their new job. They took Hannah under their wing. Like Joanna would have.

How could I have thought Tavri's tantrums were cute? How pathetic I must seem to the others, a male so blinded that his own mate tried to have him killed and he still denied it. Joanna doesn't deserve such stupidity. And while I cannot argue with King Brachard over being the one to bring Joanna to Mont Grove, I can only hope that the trip is far enough in the future that she and I can be cordial with each other, especially if there are new males in her bed.

I ignore the searing pain in my gut at the thought of her sharing with others what she's given to me.

"Do you agree, Latsil?" Brachard bellows. "You will bring Joanna to see the mountains?"

"Aye." I agree without looking up, knowing his shouting voice is normal for him.

"Good, good," Brachard continues, as if pleased that I'm not going to argue. How can I? He turns his attention to Kreele.

"Kreele, I didn't see you come back after walking Joanna home. Did you stay the night with one of our whores?" Brachard asks slyly.

I freeze and for the first time, look at Joanna to catch her expression. All four whores look frozen in place but there's something oddly wrong with Joanna. Horror? Guilt?

When I look at Kreele, I definitely see guilt.

"Aye, I did," Kreele responds but his voice is reserved. Wary.

He was with Joanna. The three orc whores knew it, that's why they buffered Joanna between them.

Cold fury washes through me.

Just like Kreele protected his sister when she hated Tavri, Bessica protects Kreele when she knows he fancies Joanna. It didn't matter that the horny bastard knew I wanted her.

And I left Joanna vulnerable enough to already pick another. Part of me resents her for allowing him to touch her but then again, I know he came at her when she was vulnerable. He is the male in the wrong, just as he was before.

I ignore the small voice that says it was Tavri who initiated his attention.

King Brachard looks back and forth from me to Kreele—and then looks to Terk. I know he's remembering the drama between us during my mating with Tavri.

Brachard clears his throat. "Who was the—"

Joanna interrupts him. "When he walked me to my cabin, one thing led to another."

The entire room goes quiet.

I'm not sure if my heart is broken or if I'm in shock when I snarl, "I thought you were interested in Terk."

My heart stutters as I watch her take a deep breath before she answers me.

The well-trained Joanna leans back and winks, then smiles at me. The look makes my heart gallop even faster, threatening to explode from my chest.

"A whore may have many interests," she says. "That is the beauty of the job."

"Aye," I say softly.

It's not Joanna I'll take to task. It's Kreele... then Terk. This is history repeating itself, but this time I will never trust my brothers again.

"In any case," Brachard continues. "We will celebrate this eve. Bring out the instruments and the ale, we will have song and dance way into the night."

I stand and push back my plate, leaving it on the table.

It's later, when the bonfire is started and the whores all dance, when I see Terk's attention on the dancers. Like Kreele, does Terk also focus on Joanna? I think he has not dropped her from his interest since the day I saw them walking together before we went to Creede. I should make an excuse to leave and avoid the torture, but my body is tense and needs the release of a fight.

My chance comes when he lifts an empty barrel of ale to take back to the kitchens, I follow him, which is not unusual. Oftentimes, males carry a full barrel back together.

He's in the cellar, taking too long to pick another, when I head down the wide, stone steps.

"Latsil." He grunts in surprise when I stop in front of him.

"You knew how I felt about her," I say quietly. "Every single one of you knew from the day we entered her diner in Granby."

"It's not what it looks like—"

I raise my brows at his obvious lie. "I didn't catch you flirting with her the morning we went to Creede?"

"Flirting, aye. But that doesn't mean I was going to do anything else."

There's still something sneaky on his face and so I hit him. With a grunt, he goes down and then I'm on him. He strikes out a beefy fist and hits me in the eye, but it barely fazes me in my rage. I hammer him with my fists, hoping Joanna won't be attracted to him when he's as ugly as me. I hear running footsteps in the halls upstairs and then a familiar voice.

"Latsil! Stop!"

I pause, and Terk gets one in. My head snaps back, but then I snarl when Joanna places herself between two raging orcs.

But it's fine. Terk steps back also, his hands balled into fists, his nose bleeding.

I'm so angry I'm shaking. "Do not put yourself in harm's way, Joanna."

"*You* don't put me in harm's way, Latsil," she says quietly.

I freeze. She's right, I didn't think of her when I stalked her lover to the cellar. I didn't think she would follow, nor did I think she would place herself between us to save him.

My shoulders slump as I realize it's over. I've lost her. When she said she wanted to be a whore, she meant it. I'm not special to her, she wants the attentions of other males.

"I-I'm sorry, *m'kirn*. Terk, I apologize for—"

"No," he says. "I can't take this." He looks over at Joanna who stares at him with wide eyes. "Latsil, I wasn't trying to entice your female into my bed. Joanna caught me in Bessica's tent and has been covering for me. I never thought it would cost her relationship with you over it."

Terk and Bessica?

I have to forcibly snap my jaw shut.

"Then it should be you and Kreele in here brawling," I say.

He winces. "Aye. It won't be long. The secret's out now."

"How long has this been going on?"

"Shortly after you falsely accused us of it."

Now it's my turn to wince. "Again, I'm sorry I caused the rift between you and Kreele."

He nods, jaw tight. "It's done. I forgave you for it long ago. But you see why she and I can't come out with it now. Kreele will believe those old rumors were true back then, even when we both denied it. I can't have Bess upset because her brother thinks she lied."

"I won't say a word," I vow. "It's not my place."

"Then what is your place, Lats?" Joanna asks. "To follow a man and jump him in a cellar for being with me when you don't want to be? When you already know I have the right to be with any male I wish?"

"I'm not sure," I admit.

"If it had been Kreele in the cellar, would you have jumped him?" she asks.

"Aye," I admit, the shame making me hang my head. "He was next."

"And yet you don't want me?" she asks.

"I don't deserve you. Obviously," I say wryly.

"Then let me make it easy for you," she says. "Take me to Creede and drop me off there. I'll sew for a living and sell my dresses in the mart."

I can't do anything but stare at her, aghast. It's a good solution. I wanted her gone, did I not? Creede is safe enough and there, she won't be a whore. I won't have to live each torturous day wondering which male she pleases through the night. She'll be among her own kind. But I can't speak, I can't process, I can't do anything but panic that I won't be able to see her again.

"You can take me, or I'll find someone else who will," she says when I remain silent. Then she sighs, turns, and stomps up the stairs, leaving me clutching my chest like a fool.

"Why don't you just tell her you love her?" Terk asks.

"What does an ugly brute like me have to offer her?"

"A cabin? Wealth? Love?" He sighs. "Because that's not you talking, fool, asking why you're not good enough. That's Tavri."

I finally tear my gaze from the steps where Joanna left.

"Tavri's dead."

"And good riddance. We've been tiptoeing around this problem for long enough. She wasn't good for you, and she wasn't good for the clan. She brought you down and tore us all apart. I know you loved her and I'm sorry you have to hear this, but we all suffered so that you could find happiness with your mate. It just wasn't meant to be."

"Aye. I'd come to the same conclusion recently during the time I spent with Joanna."

"Then stop letting old patterns make you unhappy. Since Joanna's been here it's like we've had our old Latsil back. The one we knew before Tavri. That's how I know Joanna is good for you, so don't let her get away."

"You heard her admit that she was with Kreele."

"So what? That means nothing. You just thought she and I were together."

"She admits to it."

"So? She might've said she was with me if she felt it was necessary to cover up the relationship between me and Bess."

After we hug it out, it's like we both notice what a mess we are. I start straightening my torn tunic and Terk starts brushing the dirt off my back. I use the corner of his shirt to wipe the smeared blood from his upper lip and then gag when he takes his finger, licks it, and dabs at a spot near my cheek.

He grins and sticks his wet finger in my ear, which makes me shove him. Then we grab a barrel and carry it back, feeling everyone's eyes on us.

By the time I head back out to where the others dance, Joanna won't look my way and Kreele glares at me. The evidence is on my face, along with Terk's. King Brachard looks disgusted as he looks between our bruised faces. I feel like skulking underneath a table and hiding out from the world.

I try my hardest to get close to Joanna, but she thwarts my every move. I finally corner her into a dance but because of my luck it is a fast-paced one where I cannot hold Joanna close the way I intended. I cannot whisper in her ear to apologize for being such a fool. I cannot beg her to stay.

But first thing tomorrow I intend to do all of that.

Chapter Twelve

Joanna:

"Get to the main building! All of you. If you notice anyone missing, let the guard know who it is." The gruff old male is missing the pointed end of his tusk as if it had been broken off in a brutal battle.

"What? What is going on?" Grunalda asks.

"Princess Hannah has been kidnapped by Blackhearts. Now move! Everyone."

There's no more information as we're all rounded in through the kitchens. And there I discover the very same cellar where Latsil and Terk fought is an underground cavern for hiding.

Down there already is Aga, Brun's mother.

"Pipsqueak, come sit," Vinshesa says, pulling me in front of her. She loosens my hair, combs through it with her fingers and begins to braid it. She's nervous and needs something to do with her hands so I sit still and let her.

"Ogol was on guard duty," Aga says. "He alerted us that Blackhearts grabbed Hannah and took her down river, then he followed. Brachard and Brun's royal guard are in pursuit."

"Why would they think they can get away with this?" Bessica asks.

"I'm sure they'll claim some sort of trickery, much like they did when Latsil was kidnapped."

"This may make Latsil recall his dark times in captivity," Aga says, her eyes on me. "We must remember to be patient with him."

95

Is that what Latsil's attitude has been about? First to push me away and then to exhibit such jealousy he fights with his own friends?

"When Latsil came back from the orcs to heal, scarred and bruised, Tavri told him over and over again how ugly he was. And to add insult to injury, she became interested in my brother," Bessica says.

"Sometimes when a male is told often enough that he's ugly, he begins to believe it," Aga agrees. "Especially by the one who is supposed to love him."

I keep to myself that I think Latsil's problems began when I came to the village. I think he was better off without me reminding him of his dead mate. And just as quickly as we were rounded up into the cellar of the main building, we're told it's safe to leave. Everyone bounds upstairs and out of the building. A cheer erupts when prisoner orcs are dragged straight to the stocks.

"Aga! Aga, my love," King Brachard bellows.

The queen runs across the yard and throws herself into his arms. "Brachard! How is Hannah? Is she safe?"

"Aye. We fished her out of the river and captured the ones responsible. Brun has taken her to his tent for a hot bath."

He looks to Bessica, Grunalda, and Vinshesa. "Give them a few minutes and you can tend to her. We are leaving for Serenity soon."

"Serenity? Why?" Aga asks.

"The orcs who captured her said she was sold to them and not Brun. We must speak to Lord Montierge to see who has concocted this wild scheme with the Blackhearts. And to warn him that they are headed toward his village to collect the gold they paid for her." He turns toward a guard. "Forty guards have been sent to intercept the Blackhearts. If there are more than twenty in their raiding party, our team may not return. But if the information the captured orcs have given us is true, there will be less than that, and our males will return safe and sound. When they do, send the team back to Serenity to meet the rest of us."

"May I go too? With them?" I ask quickly, before I can lose my nerve.

"We all should," Bessica says. "Hannah will need us."

"Aye," the king says thoughtfully. He turns behind him and says to one of the guards "Have Terk stay behind. He will lead the last batch to Serenity and will bring the whores."

I can't help but feel that the king is deliberately breaking up Latsil and Terk because of the fight. I hope that Latsil doesn't pick another fight with Kreele when I tell him I intend to stay behind in Serenity.

No one notices how quiet I am as we near Granby, but Terk lets me ride with him on his horse. I feel bad because this could be some time for him and Bessica, but she winks and shakes her head like she wants me to think that would be too obvious.

Terk must feel it when I tense up on the road that passes by Granby because he whispers in my ear. "Shh, little one. You have been strong and brave, leaving behind everything you know and making your way into the world by yourself. There is no reason to fear now, not with an army surrounding you."

I try to relax my muscles. "Aye. I guess I'm just stressed because"—I take a deep breath, pretty sure he'll keep my secret since I kept his— "I'm going to stay in Serenity. And I hoped there wouldn't be any disappointment from the girls, or another scene with Lats. He may blame Kreele this time."

"I'll handle the girls. And I think they would surprise you. I'll support you any way I can on one condition."

"Oh?"

"Mmm. You talk to Latsil *before* you tell anyone else."

"I can do that, I guess."

"Then you have nothing else to worry about, *m'kirn*. I promise."

He squeezes his arms around me and releases, like a mini-hug, and I pat his hand where he holds the reins. I was so lucky to have made the great friendships I did in Solaya. Though short, it was the best time of my life, and I will miss it greatly.

After two more breaks and listening to Grunalda complain about how much her ass hurts, we finally arrive in Serenity to find a beaming Hannah with Brun next to her side. Lord Montierge stands with King Brachard, who breaks away when he sees the rest of us.

"Tie the horses in the stables," he calls out. "We are planning a human wedding! Joanna, get with Latsil. Hannah needs someone to find some sort of flower in the woods and you probably know what it is."

I nod, wondering how awkward it'll be with Latsil. But then Terk trots us to a small grove of trees and there he is, standing tall and watching us all. He moves to the horse and his hands wrap around my waist to pull me down. My legs nearly collapse when my feet hit the ground and he tightens his arm, holding me against him until I have some strength in the muscles.

Terk leaves us, dismounting and walking the horse to the stables.

"Are you all right?" Latsil asks and Gods fire, I'd forgotten how deep his voice is. How it sends pangs of longing shooting straight through me.

"Aye, just need a bit of stretching." I grimace when I realize how that sounds... like I want to stretch by wrapping my legs around him.

"Joanna," he blurts out. "I've missed you so much. I'm a jealous fool for thinking you were with Terk or Kreele."

I sigh. "Latsil, I understand. Your ex-mate, she was interested in Kreele, wasn't she? No wonder you thought I would be. Especially since I implied as much."

"The truth is, *cara'jek,* I didn't want to tie you to a male who can't make good decisions. And I couldn't make them. I trusted her when no one else did."

"That's not on you. That's on her. Tell me, Lats." I step up on my tiptoes to bring myself closer to his lips. "How does the rest of your clan feel about me? Do they think I might sell you to the Blackheart orcs?"

"No! the entire clan loves you. King Brachard invited you to Mont Grove, didn't he? He never allowed that before."

But I'm not sure. "I-I'd planned to stay here, Lats. In Serenity. That's why I asked the king if I could come along."

His jaw drops. "But your cabin—"

"It's your cabin."

"I built it so you would feel safe." He winces, knowing I walked in on the fight between him and Terk.

"I couldn't feel safe when I make you uncomfortable with my profession—"

"I'll learn to live with it, *cara'jek*. I promise. I'd rather have you nearby, even if I have to watch you with others."

But do I have to take others? So far, I haven't. So far, every other orc has stayed away from Latsil's whore.

"What does *cara'jek* mean, Latsil?"

He cups my jaw in his hand. "In your language, it translates to *beloved*. Or *sweetheart*. Or something more possessive like... *mine*."

His? He was calling me his?

"Joanna!" Hannah comes running up, Brun right at her side. "Did you meet my father? Lord Montierge, meet Joanna, one of my best friends."

"Sir." I curtsy, the way I always thought I might when I met Hannah's father. Plus, she called me one of her best friends. I'm back to my life being nearly complete.

Mayhap I can stay in Solaya. It may be all right, after all.

"Joanna, 'tis my pleasure," Lord Montierge says, with a deep bow.

Hannah fingers one of my braids. "Vinshesa's?"

"Aye. You can tell?"

Hannah giggles. "Yes. She makes them smaller than Bessica, and tighter than Grunalda. Look, twins!" She waggles her own braid, holding it against mine and sure enough, they're the same size.

I can't help but smile.

"I know you just got here, but do you think you can head back into the forest to find me a laurel tree for some mistletoe? I wanted mistletoe in my bouquet as a child and I think it'll be a nice touch."

"Of course, it will!" I grin widely at the whimsical idea. "I'll find you one and make a beautiful bridal bouquet!"

"I'll take her," Latsil says quietly. "We'll take a carriage so she can arrange your flowers."

"Thank you both so much," Hannah says, and her eyes are sparkling with happiness.

I'm sure mine are too because right now, I have Latsil.

He pulls the carriage as deep as it'll go into the forest, then helps me out of the front seat so we can walk.

And he holds my hand. It's sweet and amazing to walk through the beautiful, if nippy, woods with his larger hand holding mine. When I find what we're looking for, we pick bundles and put the cuttings into a basket to take to the wagon. We've brought vases of water, all standing tall into other baskets, and pick as many wildflowers and leafy vines on thin branches for decoration that I can twist together.

"Will you ride back home with me? Instead of with Terk?"

I can't believe he needs to ask. "On one condition."

His lips tighten. "Ask it."

"Kiss me, please."

For such a large male, I'm surprised at how quickly he can move. It's like he's afraid I'll change my mind if he gives me any pause at all. Or like he's been waiting for this moment for so long and he can't believe it's here.

Very delicately, he cups my jaw in his hands, running his thumbs along my jawline, tilting my head up to receive him. His gaze searches mine all the time he lowers his head, taking his time, and I'm aware of everything. The soft brush of his beard against my chin. The firm touch of his lips, the tenderness of his hands. The way he's not breathing, as if he's anticipating everything that's me.

Rising up on my toes, I shove my hands onto his thick shoulders and open my mouth to his.

One of his arms wraps tight around my waist and he hauls me up against his broad chest. I feel tiny against him, like a doll, and as cherished.

His tongue hungrily sweeps past my lips, devouring my mouth like a starved man. With every stroke, my heart pounds and pleasure zings through my veins. The kiss is everything delicious I've missed about him, his taste, his scent, his touch.

A desperate moan rolls up my throat and I try to press closer, except there's no room, not with the clothing between us. And yes, I've attained true whore status because there's nothing more I'd admit to than wantonly needing our naked skin together and his cock plunging deep inside me.

"Lats, please, I need you so much," I finally pull away to gasp.

"*Cara'jek*, I must feel your cunt stretched tight around me, gripping me and squeezing as you come."

His voice, dripping with need, makes me shiver. I fumble a bit with the ties of his leathers, working them loose to free his gorgeous cock. When I grip it in the palm of my hand, he's hot and hard.

"Let's get stark naked and fuck in the woods, aye?" I ask, watching the lust flare in his eyes.

"Of all times not to be wearing a skirt," he complains. "I could sit you right on my cock, wrap your legs around my hips."

"Aye, but it's not easy to ride on Terk's horse with a skirt," I tease.

He growls. "Nay, no skirts with Terk. No skirts with anyone but me."

As he talks, he carries me to the wagon where he sets me on the edge. Two thick fingers work into the top of my waistband and tug the soft leather down my hips before he peels them down the length of my legs. Then he leans me back, separating my ankles and bending my knees to expose me to him. He studies the view, breathing hard, his hard cock still bobbing between us. He rubs his cock against my seam, but he doesn't slide in yet. Instead, he smears the head around my slick, as if testing my readiness.

"So wet for me," he says. "Without foreplay."

I give a sharp laugh. "You are the foreplay, Lats. All I do is think of you and the stirrings start inside me."

His mouth covers mine, opening my mouth with his, and the fat head of his cock presses into my opening. I'm so slick, my labia part and allows him right in. I gasp and tilt my hips, needing him deeper, needing him wedged inside me.

His tongue plunges into my mouth the same time his cock fills me to the hilt and it's so wonderful, so perfect, I don't even mind that we're still partially dressed. All I can focus on is the pistoning of his hips, the stroking of his tongue, the racing of my heart and when I come, it's magical starbursts as I release, my muscles quivering as I scream out his name.

And normally an orc pulls out of a whore when he comes, but Latsil forgets I'm just a whore, I guess, because he floods me with liquid heat and presses kisses all over my face as he pales and apologizes.

"Oh, baby, don't be sorry. I love it, Lats. I love"—I take a deep breath, aware this is wrong, aware I shouldn't admit it, but unable to stop— "you. I love you."

"*Cara'jek*, my heart. I love you too. I never knew it could feel this way, but I know now that I would have made that trip to Granby again and again just to get a glimpse of you. You were meant for orc life."

Chapter Thirteen

Joanna:

To my surprise, the vicar who conducts the marriage between Hannah and Brun is none other than the same one the merchant at Creede told me about. I've only seen him a couple of times; his wife was always present on those outings. She no longer stands at his side, and though I have Latsil across from me where he stands with Brun, I quake slightly though I'm not sure the vicar recognizes me. Why should he? Homer never had our marriage blessed. As the ceremony goes on, I start to feel a little better, though I notice Lats keeps his gaze fixated on me. He's probably wondering if a marriage brings back horrible memories and I'll need to reassure him later when we're alone.

For now, I give him a smile and dammit if my lip doesn't quiver... I immediately sober so I don't look the fool.

After Brun and Hannah kiss, Latsil comes and takes me into his arms, then we walk behind them down the aisle to leave.

The rest of the wedding is perfect as our people mill about and afterward, we mingle in the courtyard while food is brought out. We'll have just a few nibbles, sure the food is safe because the appetizers are shared by Hannah's father himself. He has a new allegiance with King Brachard, and whatever happened between Hannah and her father regarding her arranged marriage seems to be in the past since she's married to the love of her life. Afterward we will all ride back to Solaya. We'd toyed with the idea of staying in the motel in town, but because the alliance is so new, I think Brachard would rather get home until the town gets used to needing our protection.

Especially when the brother of the man accused of helping brand Hannah is dragged through town on his way to the jail. He's the black-smith and I recognize him as Granby does dealings with him also. He's marched through the center of town toward the jail. Everyone grows quiet as the human procession comes by, but the man glares at Hannah.

"You!" he snarls. "You're the reason why Elias is dead."

Hannah holds her head up, the true lady that she is. "No. I'm not. I never asked Elias to brand me in the jail with the iron you made. You and your brother are responsible."

"Look away or lose an eye," Brun snarls at him. "Because I am the one who snapped your brother's head right off his neck. I am curious to see if yours is any flimsier."

The prisoner is pulled away by the guards and Brachard and Lord Montierge make their way to us.

"The Blackheart orcs will insist on payment for the lack of the bride they thought they paid for," King Brachard says to Brun.

"Then they'll get Amos Glynnis as payment," Lord Montierge says.

"Aye," Brachard says. "That's clever. Sometimes other orc clans keep prisoners to work off debts and his brother must have bartered Hannah for information from them. I think he was going to pretend we stole her to cause a war between the two clans, never realizing who he was up against."

"While he and his brother made off with their gold and left us all behind in their mess," Lord Montierge says. "If it's not found, Amos will work off their debts for Serenity and when there's no more use for him, the Blackhearts will give him the same fate as his brother."

I'm so distracted I barely notice new riders enter the front gates that mark the town, but no one worries since they look human. At least, it never dawns on me to worry. Not until I hear my name called.

"Joanna!"

God's fire. I know that voice. Dread curdles in the pit of my stomach, and my limbs shake in full force. Slowly I turn, preparing for who I'll find.

Homer McLinn, in all his finery, stands before me like a ridiculously dressed peacock, with plumes jutting from his cap and his chest puffed out.

"Homer."

"Where have you been?" Without thinking, perhaps because it was so common for him, he grabs my upper arm, giving it a squeeze hard enough to make me squeal. It seems I'm no longer used to pain.

"Release her or lose your hand!" Latsil snarls from behind me and I can feel his fury like a wave of heat.

Homer drops my arm like a hot potato. Everything is quiet as the others come to stand with us. I wait until everyone is still before I answer my husband.

"I have been living with the orcs, sir," I say, and I'm quite proud of the way my voice rings out. There's no apology, and there's practically no fear. Not with Latsil nearby.

The vicar's eyes widen. "This was your new bride stolen by orcs?"

King Brachard looks from me to Latsil.

"These orcs did not steal me," I say. "They rescued me from the Blackheart clan. I chose to stay with them, just as I choose to remain with them. I won't go back to Granby."

"You can't," Homer says. He looks to the vicar. "This is my wife." His voice sounds churlish, as possessive as a four-year-old.

"Nay," I protest and then look at the vicar myself. "Our wedding was never blessed, sir. I'm sure his current marriage is."

That makes the vicar panic. It doesn't appear he wants his ex-wife back, and more than likely Homer has gotten a good taste of the peevish whip of her tongue. I'm sure she's not free labor in his diner either. If I were brave enough, I'd ask who cleaned up the mess I left behind.

"'Tis right," the vicar says. "Your first marriage was not sanctioned."

Homer's eyes widen. "But—"

Lord Montierge steps in. "The vicar has spoken," he says to Homer. "You may be mayor of your town, which is recognized by your people, but you're in my town now and our rules apply here. Now, your blacksmith is indisposed so take your business elsewhere. Go back home, for all I care, because you interrupted a private function."

King Brachard turns to Latsil. "Take her. She's ours," he says simply.

I turn and give Homer my back, trusting that Latsil will protect me from what I can't see. We head straight for the stables and mount Pegasus, then trot slowly through town as we wait for the others to catch up. I lean back onto Lats, his strong chest and arms the constant comfort I'm used to.

I have the pleasure of seeing the recognition in Homer's eyes as he sees the payment in the form of Pegasus I took for myself and my orc protector. And coward that he is, he keeps his lips tightly smacked together as Latsil and I ride on his horse.

Leaning back against his chest, I'm able to release the tension from the ride up, because I can't relax with Terk the same way. And Latsil's arms feel so good around me, so perfect.

Because we started our ride home late in the day, we stop to stay the night in the woods. It's nothing like the camping I did the night I was captured by the Blackhearts. These orcs have lived on the land and know what to eat, what areas are safer than others, what wild animals to look for. They're always mindful, watching for signs of other orcs, which is how they'd come upon me the first night I'd escaped.

Latsil dismounts from Pegasus first, then helps me down. One of the others takes the reins for us; Azorr's taking his horse to a nearby creek and will take ours with him. Lats walks me to where Hannah, Aga, and the other three ladies wait while the males make plans. They'll decide who'll hunt, who'll take the first shift on guard patrol, who will build a fire. They've done this many, many times because it's not long before canteens of water are passed around and we're sitting around the fire with rabbit roasting on tender green branches.

"My father told me there is a new breed of tomato with a shorter maturity season," Hannah says. "When he travels to Okrah, he'll grab seeds for us. No more losing tomatoes when the snow comes early because we'll have eaten our fill for months beforehand."

"That would be wonderful," I say. "Less canning too. Though, others have had good results in drying the tomato strips. They tend to sweeten a bit and taste a little tart."

"I'm not sure I would like them dried," Grunalda says.

"They're remoistened in olive oil. Used as a seasoning, mostly."

Brachard checks the first skewer of meat, adds a bit of salt, and sets it aside to cool. "So, tell me, Joanna. How did you end up married?"

Everyone's eyes are on me and Latsil runs his hand up my back, giving me quiet support.

"My parents died in the last orc attack. I was all alone, the crops of our farm burned, and the land reclaimed by the town. Homer McLinn stepped up and said he would be mayor and would need a wife. He grabbed my arm and I protested, but the townspeople said it was a fine choice. He needed a wife and I needed someone to keep me fed. That night, Homer told me he wanted me to run his diner from now on because he had important mayoral duties to attend." I stop, hoping the entire story is told.

"What duties were those?" Brachard asks quietly, and I can't tell if he's upset with me. He usually barks roughly but this quiet voice is somehow scarier than when he bellows.

"He-he met with the Blackhearts and agreed to a living tax. We would pay them to leave us alone. And... and that's all I ever saw him do. Sometimes he would strut about the town and visit with the working folk, many who were rebuilding the town. Sometimes he would come into the diner and make sure I ran it properly. Count the money in the till, usually." Cuffed me once when money was missing, and I made sure never to sneak some again.

"Did you ever think to escape?" he asks.

"He caught me sneaking money once, which is why he counted the till himself. Started charging me for food, too, but never paid me for working so I started to eat less and less. When Latsil and Brun and the others left for Serenity one day, while all the people of town hid in their safe rooms, I realized it was my chance to escape. Instead of notifying them that the coast was clear, and they could come out, I grabbed Pegasus and ran. But that's when the Blackhearts captured me."

"I see," Brachard says. "Forgive me for questioning you, *m'kirn*. I just need to find out what this mayor is like. What I might expect from him since he was so bold as to believe you might want to return. I needed to know if you had wanted to marry him."

"No. Never. I didn't have a choice. But I believe he thinks he is a good provider. It doesn't matter that his wife is thin or bruised. All that mattered was that I relieve him of his duties because he was exhausted and deserved an easier life."

"Every one of you orcs—and humans—are indeed lucky then to have me. I've never laid a finger on my mate."

Aga snorts as if such a thing is ludicrous.

"I make sure all are well paid for their services. I'm revered by others. In fact," the king says, "it has also been said that I have magical matchmaking abilities."

Hannah gasps and turns her head to stare at him with wide eyes. "I've never heard anyone say that."

Brachard harrumphs. "Bah. I'm sure I overheard the whisperings, and they are right! I find that I am a great arranger of marriages and matings," he says. "I solved the dilemma of my son's broken heart and gained us allies in the north where the Blackhearts rule. Is there truly nothing I can do?" he says as he pounds his chest. Around him, a few of the orcs raise their canteens in the air. "The last time there was a mating within my son's royal guard, it caused a lot of jealousy." The king looks directly at Latsil, and then Kreele, and then Terk. "I will stave off the tension between this clan this time. As I now have jurisdiction over our whores, I hereby announce the mating between Joanna, our newest human whore, and Latsil, first guard to Brun."

Everyone freezes.

Chapter Fourteen

L*atsil:*

    "What? Joanna is no longer a whore?" Normally I would rejoice to have her mine. But things were fine as they were between us, and now? Brachard just reminded her of the most hated time in her life. Being tied down to a mate. Marriage for humans or mated to orcs, she's still tied. And like she left her husband, she'll also leave me.

"Not as of now," Brachard says. "I have just decreed it."

It's not my imagination that Joanna stares at me with haunted eyes. Gods, she probably already regrets our fucking in the woods of Serenity. Had it not been for that, Brachard might not have come up with this crazy idea. I must calm her before she sneaks away in the middle of the night.

"Nothing need change, yes? You can keep your cabin. I will keep my tent." Silently, I beg her with my eyes. I beg her to stay, not to insist that I take her back to Serenity to live among the humans this very moment. Because that is the only way she can get out of mating me... to reject our king's rule by rejecting our way of life.

Brachard goes on speaking. "I am well aware of the way humans refer to whores as if they are lesser beings because they allow orcs between their legs. They have no sense to know how cherished our whores are. For that reason, Joanna must be kept safe from that weak-chinned, thin-lipped, small-dicked male who thinks she is his. We must send a strong statement that she is ours." He uses his beefy fist to strike his chest, thinking he is doing her a favor.

Everyone around the fire is quiet.

"But, of course," Brachard taps his forehead. "Latsil was mated before and still, we had issues among the guard. So, this time I'll thwart those jealousies, especially since Joanna has apparently shared her favors with Kreele and Terk."

Joanna's eyes widen and her gaze darts to the others around us, as if she's not sure if she should say something.

"Kreele." Everyone focuses on him and some look relieved that they're not called out, while Kreele is expressionless.

"It's time to become respectable. You shall be mated to..."

Only I am aware of the breath Joanna inhales.

Grunalda freezes as if she can become invisible if she doesn't breathe.

"Vinshesa."

Grunalda visibly relaxes.

"It is a gift I give this whore," Brachard says, puffing out his chest. "For we all know that I once decreed Vinshesa could never mate after the travesty she made of her last mateship. And Terk?" Brachard's eyes fall to Kreele as he speaks.

"Sir?"

"Since you and Kreele had issues in the past, I will thwart those by mating you to a whore also."

Again, Grunalda freezes. I'm not sure what anyone will do if Brachard mates Terk to her but there aren't a lot of options left. It's her or Bessica.

"Bessica. You shall mate Bessica, a clever orc with a clever tongue."

Grunalda's smile is relieved as she whispers, "Whew. I barely scraped by with the skin of my ass—"

"Grunalda!" Brachard booms. "Don't think I haven't forgotten you were part of the pact to remain a sister whore. What was the saying you three had? A whore forevermore? Forever a whore? Well, it's hardly fair that you kept your lips sealed about who came up with the idea to mate a member of the royal guard in order to pick off his mate! So, for that matter—"

"Wait. I thought we left that in the past when we were proclaimed unpaid whores," Bessica says. "Haven't we been punished enough?"

"Punished?" Brachard snorts. "You're still allowed to spread your legs and my son figured out a way to pay you anyway, aye? I wouldn't say you suffered much. Anyway, back to my brilliant matchmaking plan... Grunalda, you are hereby mated to Gorvan. A fine male who will keep you in check."

"What if we don't want to be mated?" Grunalda says.

"Well, the king knows best," Brachard says with a shrug. "I have proven that. But if you would like to refuse your mateship, remember that it's one for all and all for none. Just like your little *whore-evermore* pact. Joanna, did you swear in on that?"

Still tongue-tied, Joanna nods truthfully.

"So, if one of you refuses, I will undo the mating for all four whores and guards. And remember, Vinshesa has been banned from all future matings, so she will never again have a chance. Consider carefully because you may deprive one or two of your sister whores from the male she favors or has the chance to favor."

Grunalda's eyes narrow. Whether or not she knows of Bessica and Terk, I don't know. But she considers them, and she considers Vinshesa and Kreele, and then she looks over at me and Joanna.

Resigned, she nods her head just once.

"Well, join your new mates!" Brachard claps his hands like a youngling filled with excitement.

"Awkward," Grunalda mumbles, getting up as slowly as possible from the log to sit opposite the fire where Gorvan sits. With a glare at her new mate, she plops on the ground between his legs.

"Looks like I was awarded the cream of the crop," he says, and I can't tell whether it's sarcasm or not.

I'm too worried about Joanna, who is still frozen like a fragile bird with a broken wing. But I can't talk to her with everyone milling about.

"Don't worry," I whisper. "It'll be fine. I love you and you love me, remember? We can work through this."

Something flashes across her eyes, and I hope that it's relief. I hope that she's not worried about being tied to me. I'd never hurt her, hell, if she wanted to get rid of me like Tavri tried, I'd go willingly. For Joanna, I would.

She owns my heart.

By the time we're all ready to hit the furs, the camp is tense, but Brachard is clueless. He's whistling tunelessly and teasing Hannah about how he's sure their young will resemble him because he has such strong, wise genes.

Bessica and her brother, Kreele, are happy as larks, neither one fretting about being thrust into a mating, but that is their shared familial trait for the most part. I imagine they'll make the best of the situation, as they usually do. It is Grunalda and Joanna that are the most quiet.

When I spread our furs out and position Joanna nearer the fire for warmth, I can feel she's wary. I'm going out of my way to be extra gentle with her. I hold her close and kiss the top of her head. After a while, she snakes an arm around my middle and buries her face in my chest.

Then a rustling from across the fires catches my ear.

"Back off. I can feel your cock jutting full mast against my ass." Grunalda's voice is at full volume, and it startles the rest of us who only use hushed whispers.

But then I feel Joanna's shoulders shake and it makes me chuckle. Then Bessica starts laughing and Kreele and Vinshesa start laughing too.

"I was in a dead slumber," Brachard barks.

"Well, it is my mating night," Gorvan complains. "You can't blame a male for getting hard."

"No one wants to hear fucking on the trail," Brachard snaps. "Go to sleep and have your mating night in the village like normal orcs!"

Which makes Joanna giggle more and then Aga starts giggling and soon begins cooing to calm her husband.

By the time the sun begins to glow, we pack up camp and get ready to head back onto the trail. I open a bag of dried fruit and nuts for Joanna to snack on.

Vinshesa sees us and shoots over.

"Come on, pipsqueak. Let's go pee," Vinshesa says, grabbing my Joanna's arm.

I grunt, acknowledging that she'll keep Joanna safe without needing to thank the pesky orcen female.

But it doesn't take long for me to get Pegasus ready, and Vin and Joanna still aren't back. I make my way toward the area where they'd headed to find them wading in the stream. I wait near the trees, giving them privacy, but I can hear their voices carrying in the wind.

"Thank you for going along with the mating. Kreele and I would never have been able to be together if not for this."

Kreele and Vinshesa? How is that even possible? I think back to all the times we had downtimes in villages. He never seemed to take up with anyone. Has he been secretly in love with Vin all this time? Even when she and I were mated?

"Neither would Bessica and Terk," Joanna says.

My heart sinks. My sweet little love will go along with anything for her friends, despite her own needs. I will give her anything she wants in this mating.

"I know you're worried about Lats," Vinshesa says. "We'll help you."

"The last thing that poor male needs is another mate. Not after the last one he had. He must be having all kinds of flashbacks," Joanna says.

"I really thought I was giving you two the best chance ever by making you a whore. It was good while it lasted, aye?"

"It was the best."

"Then hold onto that. Together, you and Latsil can get through his fears."

Joanna is worried about me? She doesn't mention at all that she doesn't want to be mated to anyone. Not to her friend.

"And I worry about poor Grunalda," Joanna says.

Vin snorts. "Pfft. You should be worried about poor Gorvan. The male slept with a hard cock all night long and she wouldn't even let him lodge it against her ass."

Both females die of laughter.

"I can't believe she called him out like that. In front of everyone. Still, Grunalda is in this for all of us. Did you see her look at each of us when the king slyly reminded her that it was one for all or none?"

"Don't let her fool you, pipsqueak. Gorvan has been her crush since she was young. She won't admit it, but if you'll watch, her eyes follow him wherever he goes."

"Really?" Joanna asks.

"Aye. The only reason why she pretends otherwise is because he was the one who took her virginity—and has never been with her since. It may be a love/hate relationship, but I think this is exactly where she's meant to be."

Gorvan and Grunalda? How much have I missed out on by wallowing in my misery over Tavri's betrayal and then death? Yet none of my friends ever let me down, despite me and my petty jealousies.

"*Hiyak*," I shout out. "Everyone is packed and ready to go." I turn and head back to the camp, making my way to Pegasus.

My mate and I will have a lot to discuss on the trip home. With this mateship, I want everything laid out. I want honesty. I want love.

Chapter Fifteen

Joanna:

"Are ye comfortable, beautiful?" Latsil whispers into my ear from where he's seated behind me on the horse.

I love when his deep, grumbly voice rolls into his old accent. It shows he's deep in thought or trying hard to please. Not that he should be trying to please me, but it shows he's not lost in his past, traumatically recalling the hell of his beloved mate planning his demise with another clan.

My bottom is sore from so many hours in the saddle, for sure. It has been a rough trip but then again, I didn't plan on making the return trip back to Solaya.

"Yes, though I wouldn't mind a heated shower like we had in Creede." Unfortunately, Creede is too far south of where we're going.

"I'll heat you a hot bath in your cabin."

Does that mean he won't be with me? Will he go to his tent? "I-uh, well, are we still going to live separately then?"

Is it me or does he seem to freeze?

"Is that what you want?"

"No! I mean, before all this, before Brun had the accident, you and I went back and forth quite easily. I mean, we were comfortable in both places. I"—I take a deep breath— "I don't want to live separately."

He nuzzles the side of my neck. "I can dismantle my tent. If you want your own space, I can reassemble it near you."

My, how tongues would wag if he was relegated to the outer tent like a family pet.

"It's not necessary to reassemble."

"I want to make you happy, Joanna."

He worries that I'm unhappy? "Latsil, I am happy with you. How can I not be? I love you."

"I love you too, *cara'jek*. Ahh, but now you're *gi anyasa*, which translates to my mate, so I might call you that now and then. It's a matter of pride. I'm so proud to be the male you're mated to."

"You are? You're not having horrible thoughts that things could go wrong?"

"No, sweet. I was worried that you would hate being mated. You told me you wanted to be a whore so you'd never have to suffer through that again."

"I'm not suffering with you. I want to be mated as long as it's with you."

"You do?"

"Yes, handsome."

"I'm no longer—"

"You are. Nothing about you has changed except for a few more scars. You're the same person you were before you were captured, just like I am. Would you think I was ugly if you hadn't come upon me that first night in the woods? Because I guarantee I would carry scars from that capture. But you know what, Lats? You saved me from that fate."

"We will be happy. I think the evil old king knows what he is doing."

"I do too. He knew to pair Kreele and Vin. Bess and Terk. And look... I didn't even know about Grunalda and Gorvan until Vinshesa told me this morn."

"And none of us thought anything of the mating he arranged for Brun but look at how it happened to be to his childhood friend. I think we do have to trust that the old bastard knows what he's doing. He is king, after all."

"Aye, I am," Brachard says, passing us on his way up the trail.

That leaves us quiet for a moment.

"He has excellent hearing," I say finally.

Behind me, Latsil's body shakes with silent laughter.

By the time we see the towering stone gates that mark Solaya, a sense of homecoming washes over me.

"It's beautiful, isn't it?" Bessica asks, Terk riding behind her. He looks so happy to finally have the love of his life, to be out in the open instead of sneaking around. The sight of his utter devotion to her, lit in his eyes for all to see, takes my breath away.

"It's good to be home," I answer. I'm not as exhausted as I'd been earlier, instead I have a sense of renewed energy. Everyone does, they sit a little straighter and smiles are a little brighter.

With happy waves, we all separate—heading for our separate tents—none of us wanting to admit this is exactly what we all want. Nay, we must pretend we all hate the idea of having an arranged mateship. Three days later, Lats and I finally leave our cabin when a smiling Kreele and Terk come by to pick him up. They'd also been holed up the entire three mating days, until real life finally intervened. Latsil kisses me goodbye and mentions he'll meet me if I'd like to go eat at the main cabin for dinner.

I do a little sewing and lose track of time. The days are getting cooler, and I hurry to the building. Everywhere people mill about, setting food on the table and arranging chairs.

"Joanna! Come sit with me," Brachard barks from across the room and his voice is so loud, it's impossible to pretend I don't hear. Slowly, I make my way to his table.

"How is the mated life?" he asks as I sit on the bench next to him.

"Never better." I can't help but grin to myself as I recall the love-making this morn.

"I saw Latsil took his tent down."

"Aye, he's moved into my cabin."

"It appears all the males moved in with their mates then. But I must know, are you happy?"

"I've never been more so. I love Latsil."

"Good, good," Brachard says. "Because Hannah's father will make a visit. He's bringing his daughter some things for our brat before we make the move to Mont Grove for the winter." He raises an eyebrow. "I'll expect you to come."

I smile easily, sure I'll come, though I haven't talked to Latsil about it.

"Anyway," Brachard says, his face turning serious, "the male you married isn't giving up so easily. He insists on being brought along and I have given my permission for his visit."

"You have?" I squeak. Will the nightmare of my marriage never end? It is determined to haunt me.

He nods grimly. "He has come to present his case that your marriage was legal, and he wishes to have you back. I intend to make a case that you are happier here than you've ever been in your life."

I feel my eyebrows knit together. "I already told him I was remaining here."

"He insists on seeing for himself that you're happy. I'm sure it's an excuse, but he's willing to pay for the expedition. It seems your husband is quite wealthy." He raises his eyebrows like I should know.

"He is? I guess he would be since he never had to pay any wages." I'm aware I answer rather grumpily, and Brachard pats my hand.

"Hmm. Don't fret about it. In one moon's time we will leave for Mont Grove. There he cannot reach you no matter what he insists during this meeting. He'll find out he was quite stupid to try to bargain with orcs without doing his research."

Foolish indeed, considering he watched the blacksmith get dragged off in chains as payment for them. Another clan, but still.

"Joanna!" A voice squeals. Hannah's eyes are glowing, and her hair is loose. Behind her follow Bess, Vin, and Grunalda. "Did you hear? My father's coming. He's bringing some of my baby clothes and my cradle and even a highchair. Since he's obviously getting a carriage to haul everything, I insisted he bring more fabrics for you. We can take some to Mont Grove if you wish and leave some here in the cabin for when we return in spring."

Hannah smooths my bangs as she talks, and I love this. I love this friendship we've developed; it's even better than my childhood fantasies.

"I hope he brings plenty of fabric," I say. "Because it won't be long before I'll be making some maternity gowns." I pat her rounding belly, though it's barely a bump.

Could actually be last night's dinner, though I wouldn't dare say it.

Her smile is beatific, she's so excited for her firstborn.

"And what about you, *m'kirn*?" Brachard says slyly to me. "My grandson will need a playmate."

I gulp and smile uneasily. Latsil is the largest of the brutes—surely, he'll produce large offspring—and Hannah giggles because she can guess my line of thought. But then Vinshesa is there, and she scoots me over so she can squeeze onto the bench next to me.

"Especially since his last mate failed to provide any offspring." Brachard glowers at Vinshesa.

"I changed my mind." She shrugs. "Have you seen the size of Latsil's head? It would ruin my lady cave."

Bessica snorts.

"I would think you, our wise king, wouldn't want this one to procreate," Grunalda says, her thumb pointing at Vin.

Bessica and Hannah softly giggle. I'm pretty sure I see Brachard's mouth twitch before he barks out, "And have you spread your legs for your mate, you selfish twit?"

"Aye, I made him beg," Grunalda says smoothly. "For three days straight."

And then I know Brachard's mouth twitched as we all burst out laughing.

"My mate is in his element," Aga says from the doorway. "Surrounded by the daughters he never had."

"Aye, the gods knew I was too soft-hearted for females," Brachard agrees and Bessica gasps but doesn't call it an outright lie.

Behind Aga are the rest of our males, who immediately come and sit at the table. The only one who looks slightly awkward as he peers at Grunalda is poor Gorvan. I imagine those two will figure it out.

Someone comes up behind me.

"*Hiyak, gi anyasa,*" Latsil says into my ear.

I spin around and then reach up to kiss his lips, loving that tiny white scar across them.

"Hello, handsome. Did you work hard today?"

"Mmm, for the most part, despite missing my mate every minute. What did you do?"

"Sewed. Made you a tunic and started on some looser tunics for when Hannah's belly grows."

"Make it easy on yourself. Just cut them off at the chest and leave the belly bare. If you really like her, you can possibly stitch a hem underneath her teats."

He barely flinches when Hannah smacks him upside the back of the head.

"Well, she'll be pregnant through the winter, so it won't be naked weather," I tease.

"Naked weather is what got her in this predicament," he agrees.

"Bathing did, actually," Brun says. "I can't keep my mate out of the tub."

Hannah makes an indignant sound but then Brun starts kissing her.

"I ran into your merchant friend from Creede," Latsil says. "Her name is Rosemary."

"You did? Did she have anything interesting to say? Did you tell her I said hi?"

"I sent your well wishes. She has a niece staying with her. Abigail's her name. Azorr spent most of his time flirting with the niece while I picked you up a new color of fabric."

Azorr grumbles.

"What color is it?" The male has bought me everything under the sun.

"A shade of buttercup I think you'll enjoy."

I hold back my snort. I have never met a man who knows so many words for the color yellow, especially one whose first language isn't English. I find it endearing that my mate loves the shade.

"And a rose bush," he goes on, his voice continuing rather excitedly. "The roses are yellow. I had to have it for you. It will be beautiful against the brown of your cabin. I just wish it would have been in so I could have brought it home."

"I'll make the trip back to Creede in a few days to pick it up," Azorr says, not even pretending to give us privacy. I think he's looking for an excuse to visit Rosemary's niece. "I'll even plant it quickly before I head out to Mont Grove so when we all return in the spring, Joanna's bush will be ready."

"I appreciate your kind words, sir," I tease. "But please do not refer to my bush in the future."

A round of chuckles rolls down the males as Azorr scowls to mask his darkening cheeks.

"Aye, we're not that close for you to be so familiar with my mate's bush."

I can't help but laugh at Latsil's dry tone.

"Give the male a break," Gorvan says, and it's deliberately condescending. "He is the only unmated fool left."

"You are barely mated yourself," Azorr snaps. "Grunalda still makes you beg for it."

"She likes it like that," Gorvan responds. "It is a game between mates. You'll find out soon enough when you find a strong orc female."

"Or a sweet human female," Latsil says, nuzzling my neck.

Chapter Sixteen

J oanna:
Several weeks roll by and just as I begin to think the Serenity people have forgotten their promise to visit, we get word that their party approaches.

Homer is brought into our camp with a cloth bag over his head. The guards lead him to where we sit, and he stumbles. One shoves him when he arrives in front of King Brachard, so he drops to his knees and stays there as the bag is pulled off him.

A flash of the old familiar fear hits me as his gaze immediately seeks me out and I lean closer to Latsil.

It doesn't stay with me, however. Homer looks about the camp, noticing how Brachard glares, seeing all the orc guards surrounding him, even noticing the six orc cages all lined up in a row, each one holding a Blackheart prisoner. His eyes lock there for the span of a few seconds. His face whitens, and his Adam's apple bobs up and down. I wouldn't think he'd be so afraid of Blackhearts, considering he pays them a tax for protection.

He tries to straighten his back as if he's not terrified out of his mind, but it's there in the trembling of his fingers, the flitting of his gaze back and forth.

Curious that seeing Blackhearts locked up would bring such fear.

"King Brachard," he says, trying to deepen the high pitch of his voice. "I'm Mayor McLinn of Granby. The leader of the town," he explains as if no one here has heard the term mayor... which quite possibly they haven't.

"And what business do you have here?" Brachard bellows. "I find it annoying that I have guests here who were inconvenienced enough to need to bring you on what should have been a happy trip."

"Well, you see, Joanna is my legally wedded wife—"

"I recall! I also heard when your vicar said the marriage wasn't good."

"Well, it occurred to me since then. You see, since I am mayor, I do have the authority to proclaim marriages." He manages to look down his nose, even while on his knees. "The equivalent of your matings," he explains, as if orcs can't figure out what a marriage might be. "The marriage is legally binding. Therefore, Joanna can't possibly remain a resident of your little village." He waves his hand as if Solaya is nothing compared to a human town. "Because she is my wife first and foremost. And to compensate for the food and keep you've given her so far, I'm quite willing to pay for her care." Homer pulls out a leather bag of coin and I have to hold back a deep inhale. I know that purse, the black leather with the gold stitching and the emblem. The leather is what Blackhearts wear, with the unique gold stitching underneath their loincloths or vests. They even had their horses decorated with the colors.

That can't be a coincidence, but no one else says anything or even seems to notice. But I've seen Blackhearts three times now, and I notice.

Homer opens the drawstring and pulls out a handful of gold coins. Not a mixture of coppers, silver, and gold. All straight gold.

"That won't be necessary right now," Brachard says. "Put your purse away." He turns to me. "Joanna, are you happy with Latsil?"

I move from Latsil's side—where he sits sprawled in a chair next to Brun—to stand behind him instead. I feel better with his body blocking me and everyone else. He's safety and security all wrapped up in my handsome, powerful orc. I drop my chin onto the top of his head and wrap my arms around him, and he clasps my hands in front of his chest with his.

"I am, sir. I love Latsil."

Brachard raises his thick brows toward Homer as if to say, *see*?

But Homer goes on like an idiot. "While I understand you also wish to keep Joanna, I think we can come to a business arrangement. If you would want to deliver her to my town, I would make sure your delivery person is handed over as much gold as you ask for."

"Look at Joanna. Do you see how she loves her orc? What makes you think she would want to leave him?"

"I'm sorry, I don't understand why you think Joanna would have a choice. This is a business arrangement between you, as king of your village... and me, the mayor of my town. Name your price."

"Well, I should think about your fine offer. The decision won't be made today. I am a suspicious ruler, and I don't trust you to roam free throughout my village, Mayor McLinn. I do have a treaty with Serenity, though, so while these males visit with my clan, I need you out of the way. You will stay in one of the cages until it's time to leave. You will wear your blindfold on the way home again. And if one of my orcs shows up with Joanna on his horse, you will know I've accepted the arrangement between us. Send back all the gold you have, and I will keep the amount on the honor system, trusting that you'll give me all."

No one misses how Homer's eyes light up. He has no intention of giving Brachard all his gold. He'll give him a meager portion and claim that was everything.

But then the light dims as he notices the cages and the hungry way the Blackhearts continually study him. Because what Homer doesn't realize is they recognized the purse. They know exactly who discovered the gold they'd given for Hannah.

"Is that necessary?" Homer asks. "I assure you I am a man of my word."

"Of course, it is necessary. I have ruled," Brachard says.

Homer's eyes flip back and forth between the cages and the king. "But the cages are connected. Those prisoners will be able to reach through to my cell."

"Aye, it will be a long night for you. It appears orcs have rather long arms. Which may be why humans used to claim we ran on all fours. I imagine you will avoid the prisoner on your right side, and keep in mind the one on the left." Brachard shrugs. "You'll figure it out." With a careless flick of his wrist to our guards, two of them grab Homer by his flabby upper arms and drag him to the cage. As soon as he's inside, the Blackhearts on either side of him are completely still, though they watch him with the movement of their eyes. I think they're building his anxiety. Getting him nice and fearful right before dark. Brachard claps his hands and turns to Lord Montierge.

"Well, it's been an exciting day. You must be weary from your travels. Let us show you and your guard to your tents, and then we shall see what you brought while we eat, yes?"

Hannah's father has a huge smile also. Then it dawns on me... by Brachard showing Lord Montierge which tents they'll sleep in, they'll have privacy to discuss what's going on with Homer.

"Brun and Hannah! First Guard Latsil and Joanna." Brachard barks and Brun and Latsil move to surround our king and queen. Hannah and I stand by our mates.

The cages are still quiet when we enter the first of the tents.

"Did you see that bag?" Hannah's father asks.

So I wasn't the only one who noticed.

"Aye. I think we know where the blacksmith's missing gold went. Whether or not Mayor McLinn was aware, or he just happened to find Elias and Amos's hidden gold, I don't know. What I do know is our Blackheart prisoners are keeping quiet because they recognized what it was. I wasn't going to let them live, but this changes my mind. However, we will not release them until you are safe because right now, they will hunt your party. But we are establishing that you are protected by the West Mountain Orcs, so they have all night to think about that. Soon the dimwits will realize that they know exactly which town the mayor lives in," Brachard says.

"Ahh. Both Serenity and Solaya will be off the hook," Lord Montierge says with a nod. "The leader of the Blackhearts will realize you freed his males not out of the goodness of your heart because it was within your rights to order their deaths, but because in good faith you wish for them to recover their gold. Orc gold."

A huge smile breaks out on Brachard's face before he winks. "And it stresses that I'm protecting Serenity by allowing my connections to get home safely. I am a fair and just king that way."

My revenge comes in watching Homer run as the sun dips lower in the horizon. At first, he begins to pant as he races up and down the length of the cage, avoiding one side, then the other. Unlike the orcs, Homer doesn't have an ankle manacled with the other end of the chain staked outside the cage. Then he begins to squeal as the two on either side of him start to coordinate efforts. Brachard won't let him get caught, though. No, this is just a scare, something to prolong his tension, knowing the orcs may be freed one day, and wondering when that day will arrive. I imagine he'll leave Granby as soon as possible... but he won't get far. Brachard will release the six Blackhearts and I imagine a couple will go for Homer while the rest race home to their king to tell them what they've discovered.

Brachard will allow them to recover their gold. That is part of his plan of keeping relations up since he slaughtered half their clan, including their previous king.

They'll never forget Brachard's name. The orcs that he holds prisoner now each owe him a fealty to be paid in five years' time over the misunderstanding with Hannah. According to Brun, they touched her. I wouldn't want to be sought out by him for not paying because as much as we love our goofy king, he can be terrifying.

I'm no longer scared of Homer. I find one night of watching his psychological terror quite satisfying in relieving what he's done to me.

Because of that, I can't stop eating, knowing he's hungry and remembering all the times he enjoyed the meals I made while I starved. I'm on my second plate of spareribs, enjoying them outside with Latsil where we can pretend to watch the sunset, but really watch the action in the cages.

"Is it okay if I leave you?" Latsil asks. "I'll be watching from just inside that tent. I want to see if he's got balls enough to talk to you."

"Yes, it's fine."

As soon as he walks away, I regret my brave words. It seems even the captured orcs play with me because they decide to give Homer a reprieve.

"Joanna! Go get me something to eat," Homer barks at me, so sure I'll obey his commands even here.

"Why would I do that?" I ask him, genuinely baffled.

"Because your king and I just made an arrangement, wife. He'll be shipping you off because I have more gold than what I carry today," he hisses, patting his inner vest pocket where he carries the leather purse across his shoulder. "So be a smart girl and don't make me mad."

"Homer," I say, standing and coming closer to his cage. Slowly, I bring a rib up to my teeth and take a juicy bite of the meat. I lick my lips to catch every bit of the delicious, thick sauce that drips. "Do you remember you made me pay for my food?"

He growls and for once, it doesn't scare me. Nay, I've heard enough growls in the village to know there are things louder and more violent than the small bully locked in the cage.

"Everyone earns their keep! You should be lucky I gave you a job."

I take another bite of the ribs, moaning softly at the tender, tasty morsel. Ignoring his glare as he swallows air.

"Do you think I've gained too much weight?" I ask, scraping the bone with my front teeth.

His eyes fall on my cleavage. "You would look fine in a proper corset instead of that scandalous dress."

"I eat as much as I want here. Latsil loves my new curves. I love my new curves."

Because I have a plateful of ribs, and I'm not stupid enough to get close, I toss one into the cage next to Homer. The orc there immediately picks it up and devours it.

All five orcs come as close as their ankle chains allow.

"Here, girl. Throw one here," one begs.

I know they've been fed crusty bread, and they're lucky to have that. Brachard keeps them weak.

I figure a bout of meat—especially greasy ribs—will give them intestinal issues tonight.

"For a boon," I barter.

"Name it."

"Nay, that isn't how the mate of First Guard Latsil operates."

The orc's eyes sharpen at the mention of Latsil's name. I want him to understand who my mate is and how different I am from the first mate of Latsil's who once bartered with them.

"You will come up with a way to repay me. And *you* will send me a message one day telling me what you've done for me. Do you understand?"

This orc is clearly intelligent because he looks to Homer, his gaze settles on his breast where Homer keeps the purse underneath his vest, and nods.

"Aye, mate of Latsil of the West Mountain Orcs. You have my word."

I'm not sure how to convey that I don't want anything gross sent... like a finger or an ear. Not in front of Homer.

"Then catch."

I toss him a meaty rib and the others clamor as close as they can.

"My word too, Latsil's mate."

I toss that one a rib.

"Over here, Latsil's mate. My word is good also."

He gets one.

"Don't give them all away, you twit," Homer snips. "I told you I'm hungry."

"Mmm. Are you?" I eat another, digging from Latsil's side of the plate now.

When the other orcs also swear, I toss them the last of the meat.

"I swear, you're just as stupid now as you were when you ran my diner!" Homer screams. He reaches for the plate with my half-eaten rib on it, but I take a step back.

I'm not scared at all. I'm actually having fun.

"Yoohoo," Vinshesa says, carrying a tray. "I'm on my way to... um, that spare tent over there"—she points to where Latsil is hiding— "and wondered if you needed a refill. Can't imagine you ate all of those so fast." She pretends she doesn't see the prisoners licking their fingers.

"Aww, thanks, Vin. You're the best."

She takes my empty plate and leaves me with another one piled with ribs. This time, each are separated for me.

Guess I was never really alone. I imagine they're all watching. Wondering why I'm feeding all the prisoners and maybe assuming I'm just torturing Homer. But going hungry isn't the only torture.

"Joanna! Give me that at once!" Homer says, eyeing the heavy stack of ribs.

I pick one up, lick up one side of the rib and down the other. "Really?" I ask, wondering how far he'll go.

Not far. He glares at me.

"Put it down and pass me a fresh one."

"I'll take the licked one," says the Blackheart who'd given me the first swear.

I toss him my licked rib along with a fresh one.

All the rest of the orcs clamor for one, but they only receive one each.

Homer's sweating now, tight-lipped with anger. I imagine if we were in Granby right now, he'd probably grip me by my arm and toss me against the table.

I lick my fingers, moaning excessively again, and then toss a third round to the orcs, of course giving my first benefactor another freebie. I think he'll remember the loyalty.

Homer makes one last threat.

"If I go hungry this night, I'll make sure you go hungry for a week, you stupid—"

For the second time in my life, my mate manages to sneak up without me noticing. All I hear is a gagging sound as he grabs Homer's scraggly neck.

"Do you taste like chicken, mayor?" Latsil asks. "If you'd touched my female, I'd chop off your hand and we'd fry it tonight to find out."

But Homer can't speak because he's choking.

"Never speak to Joanna again. Do you understand?"

Homer's eyes water, tears running down his red face as he tries desperately to nod. Latsil flings him aside and he lands on his back, his fat belly up, the ridiculously ruffled shirt untucking from his trousers, leaving his stomach hanging loose and looking like the pale underside of a fish. He stays on the ground, gasping for air.

I flip out the rest of the ribs to the hungry prisoners.

"Generous love," Latsil says, leaning down to kiss my barbecue-sweet lips.

"She's the sweetest of us all," Vinshesa agrees, suddenly appearing to take the empty tray and handing me a wet cloth to wipe my sticky fingers. "Maybe smartest too." She whistles as she walks off, and Latsil looks puzzled.

I smile easily at him. He'll find out soon enough.

Chapter Seventeen

Joanna:
     The entire village erupts with laughter in the wee hours of the morn.

Homer was run ragged for hours on end, squawking like a chicken, until Brachard tired of the noise and barked at the guards to stuff a rag into his mouth. It was quite comical for those watching; the spindly legs balancing his egg-shaped body, his face red and panicked, his tiny mouth spread into an O, his hands flailing as he raced from one orc's reach to the other. Brachard told Homer that if he removed the gag and used his voice just once, he'd cut out his tongue.

Homer paid attention. So did the orcs. They seemed to perk up and I wondered if they would try doubly hard to make him squeal so Brachard would follow through.

But before the sun rose, another wave of laughter echoed around the village. It made me smile because I could guess at what happened.

"Want to tell me what I missed?" Latsil murmurs sleepily.

"Mmm," I mumble, comfortable in my favorite position on his chest. "I imagine the greasy ribs ran right through the orcs, who haven't eaten much but bread and water for days."

By the time the sun rises, it's a sight to see. The prisoner orcs had needed their rest, so they took their slop buckets and flung the filth at Homer so their own cages wouldn't stink. Or so they claimed. Pretty sure they could still smell the mess from where they were.

"Sorry about that," Brachard apologizes to Lord Montierge with a snicker, knowing he'll be the one to ride the long journey back with the shitted man.

Homer assumes Brachard is apologizing to him.

"I cannot say it was an easy night, or that forgiveness will come easy," he sniffs, like the pompous ass he's become. "But a bargain is a bargain and as long as you deliver her safe and sound, I'll make sure you're well compensated for your trouble."

I can't believe after that hellish night, Homer still thinks King Brachard will sell me.

"Aye," Brachard says easily.

Lord Montierge says, "He'll return in the carriage. It goes without saying he expected to get his horse back during this trip and didn't bring another. I doubt if any of my guard will allow him to ride double with them."

But Homer may have learned his lesson as far as Latsil goes because he starts babbling. "Well, I see Pegasus is well loved here. I'd *once* hoped for his return, but of course, his health and well-being is more important than my wishes."

Everyone is a bit more relaxed when Homer and his stench leave. I imagine Hannah's father took him straight to the cold river and doused him, and I imagine he whined the whole time. Perhaps he'll catch a cold. That would be a double whammy, to get sick and have to plan on leaving Granby with a horrible cold when he realizes I'm never coming... but that the Blackhearts are.

And one day, not long before we're scheduled to pack up to head to Mont Grove for the winter, Brachard releases the rest of the prisoners—this time, he allows me to feed them. He's a sneaky orc, probably doesn't want them to die of starvation halfway home. He wants their message and their mission to go through, but he can't show mercy by feeding them himself.

Three weeks later
        Latsil:

The woods on the outskirts of Collins, north of Serenity, is the boundary for the Blackhearts. When we arrive, Brun lights a fire, sending up the smoke signals of the old ways.

It doesn't take long before the patrolling guard is sent to investigate. To my surprise, it's Jacovi... the leader.

A new king because I took the head of their previous ruler. And while Jacovi pretends to hate me for it, it is thanks to me that he rules.

"To what do we owe this surprise?" He barks out as their horses prance about in alarm.

None of us trust the Blackhearts. While it appears we wait for them calmly, casually sitting around the fire, a second team of our males wait hidden in the trees. Should anyone draw his sword, an arrow will pierce his chest before he can unsheathe his weapon.

"King Brachard of Mont Grove wishes to make sure you are aware of his generosity in allowing your trespassers to live and return," Brun says.

"Aye, if your king was so generous as you claim, our males would not be so thin."

I stand up and move toward the light of the flames. "Need a reminder of what they could look like?" I spread my arms out and slowly turn.

Used to be, I'd have to grit my teeth to display my shame. But Joanna has made me realize that these males are envious when they study my muscled form and see the pain I was able to take during three full moons of captivity... and still slaughter their king upon my escape. There is no more embarrassment. Now I am proud to rub my strength—my survival—in their faces.

Wisely, Jacovi doesn't say anything.

"Keep in mind, they touched a royal princess," Brun says quietly. "Their captivity was mild. We didn't even take off any fingers for the violation. Generous, indeed."

"Hail to Brachard," our males chorus, knowing such loyalty isn't prevalent in the Blackheart clan.

"All right," Jacovi concedes, gritting his teeth at our salute. "Please thank Brachard for their safe return. We owe him."

He's about to turn around when one of the males to his right—one of those we'd captured—trots his horse up. He pulls a small pouch from his saddlebag and tosses it to me. "For your mate. She asked for a boon."

I catch the pouch with one hand and nod.

"Tell her the male bargained to sell her to us if we promised to take the gold and leave him alone. Said she should be back in his keep within the next moon if we'd give him some time and the female would be ours."

"Does he live?" I ask. While I don't think they would have let him—after all, they were tricked by humans by pretending to sell their own females once before—I need to make sure so I can display his head on a post in the town where he ruled. It will be a reminder to others.

"Nay. We explained that we were there because of her, and he'd made a grave mistake in speaking against her. Before he could ask what the punishment was, we cut out his tongue."

I nod again, knowing we will visit Granby on the way home to make sure.

But then the male surprises me. "We recognized him, ye know."

I tilt my head, confused at first, but then I remember the day they were caged, holding perfectly still as Homer was locked up, following his movements with their eyes and nothing else. "Aye, you saw the coin purse. It was clearly marked as Blackheart funds."

He shakes his head. "Before that. He'd made a deal with us to invade their town and burn the outlying fields, including the homes there. Said he'd make sure the female who lived in one of those homes would be busy in town that day and she'd become his wife once he became leader. And then he'd pay us for our service each moon afterward. Which he was paying, but when we saw the coin purse, we realized he double crossed us and was paying us out of our own missing money. Nobody crosses Blackhearts."

Technically, he didn't. It was his own people he double crossed, using their money as tax to pay the Blackhearts for burning their town. Mayhap he found the blacksmith's purse later, after seeing him dragged off in chains—knew where to look since he used to do business with him—and thought he'd keep the gold.

Once the Blackhearts leave, we travel through the dark to Serenity. We will stay the night there with our allies and leave for home in the morn. But when dawn's light shines and the early morning market bustles with life, we find we don't need to go to Granby. It seems that most of their town has fled to Serenity.

Lord Montierge verifies what we suspect. The townspeople were already wary of their leader. First the imposed tax for protection, then the mayor's sudden wealth and his bride's disappearance. When the Blackhearts left their leader staked in pieces in the middle of town, too many of the villagers decided they would not wait for orcs to return and demand the tax. Rumors already swirled that Serenity had an alliance with a different orc clan, so they came to Lord Montierge.

So, after spending some time at their market, I box up Joanna's new fabrics along with a surprise—a new sewing machine that I had Lord Montierge collect from one of his traveling merchants. I want her to have one at Solaya and one at our home in Mont Grove without hauling both back and forth.

We ride home without stopping, eager to get home to our mates. Once we arrive, our first order of business is to care for the horses.

I finish brushing Pegasus and lovingly pat his flank. "There you go, brute. Let me go tend to the missus now, eh?"

He whinnies as if he understands and trots off to join the others.

I wash up quickly, getting most of the dust from the trail washed away in no time. By the time I enter the main cabin, the other males are already there.

"Latsil!"

Joanna's eyes light up when she sees me. My gorgeous mate comes running across the room to fling herself into my arms.

"Ahh, beautiful, I missed you," I say, picking her up and spinning her around. She seals her mouth to mine, and I love this. I love that she loves me.

"You have a package," I murmur against her lips, unwilling to tear myself away.

"I do? From who?"

I set her down to her feet and hand her the small, fabric wrapped present. "The Blackhearts."

She freezes midreach and I angle my head curiously. Behind us, a couple of the males snicker.

"Don't pay attention to them, sweet." I glare at the fools over my shoulder. "You may take it."

"I just—well, I'm hoping it's not going to be a finger. Or a nose."

Now the idiots who've come to surround us are full out laughing.

"*M'kirn*, you were so sweet before you mated this brute! Now you expect toes and fingers in a box?" Kreele asks.

"She said noses, fool," Terk says, and the two erupt into heady laughter again.

"It's safe, *gi anyasa*," I whisper. "The box would have stank like your husband did the last time you saw him if it was body parts." I do not tell her I peeked because of my concerns that it would be pieces of tongue.

"Ex," she corrects, instantly relieved, and then opens the small, wrapped package.

She gasps when she sees the gold coin. "Orc coin!" she exclaims. "One, two, three, four... a coin from each of the prisoners we had in captivity!"

"You were a whore rolling in gold and now you're excited over a few more coins?" Grunalda teases.

"Well, technically I only had one client."

"And I gave you all my gold," I remind her. "You *were* rolling in gold, cara'jek."

She grins happily at me. "But this gold. This means something different."

"What does it mean?" Bessica asks.

"This means they found Homer. They retrieved their own stolen gold."

"And it means they paid for the ribs you fed them," snickers Vinshesa and we all start laughing again.

"I do hope Homer didn't suffer *too* much," Joanna says, peering up slyly from her lashes.

From behind us, the king and queen had approached. Brachard grunts, making my mate spin around in surprise.

"Huh. Spoken like a true bloodthirsty orc. He deserved what he got, sweet Joanna. When my gestating daughter is not present, we will give you details." He motions with his hand toward Hannah.

From Brun's arms, Hannah does look pale, her face tinged with green as her morning sickness hits.

The other males raise their hands to Brachard and cheer.

"Let us celebrate this night and tomorrow we will pack up and head back to the mountain home, eh? The ones who will stay at Solaya will enjoy some peace and quiet."

As the others bring out the ale, I pull my Joanna onto my lap and speak softly, for her ears only. "Sweet, I have some bad news to share."

Her fingers come out to smooth my brow as the smile drops from her face, replaced by concern for me. "What is it, handsome?"

"The Blackhearts did not attack your village. Nor was your town paying them for protection. Homer petitioned the orcs to burn half of it down, including the outlying farms. He wanted to make sure you were left alone so he could step up as mayor and choose you as his wife."

She stills and her face looks stricken. "That must be why he delayed me that day, keeping me in the stables when I was to return home, when I could have warned my parents! And right before I was to leave, someone rang the church bells as an alarm when they saw the smoke from the outlying farms, and I couldn't go. They held me back from the fires."

"Aye. For their service, he agreed to make payments to the Blackhearts each full moon."

"The tax? It wasn't protection? He was collecting from us to pay them for slaughtering us?"

I nod. "I'm sorry. Had I known, I would have locked him in their cages instead of letting him have his own."

"That man killed my parents. And half the town." She's quiet for a few moments.

I tuck a strand of hair behind her ear, letting her know I'm here for her.

"Did they make him suffer?" she asks.

I nod again. "And they told him it was for you. For Latsil's mate, they said."

"Good. Then he didn't get away with it. I'm glad." She drops her forehead to mine, in the way of our people.

She has become full orc, this amazing female. The love of my life.

Then she surprises me again with her next words. "Now, handsome orc, dance with your mate. We will celebrate Homer's demise."

I grin as we stand, and she leads me to where the drummers and flutists play music.

Epilogue

Five years later:

"Aunt Jo-Jo, she's so beautiful."

At five years of age, my best friend's son, Bakog, is entranced with my three-month-old daughter. For one so young, he's already showing signs of being protective, just like his father, Brun.

Hannah and I were pregnant together this time. I was halfway through mine when she got pregnant for the second time. I swear, the two of us couldn't even take a walk without Latsil and Brun following us "at a respectable distance" to make sure we were safe.

Bakog leans down and presses his little green lips to her forehead. He's much darker than Shalia, especially with her hair being so light.

"Oh, her hair smells so good! What do you use, Auntie Joanna?"

"Lilac flowers. Next time your Uncle Lats goes to Creede, he's going to grab me a small bush. We'll plant some hedges."

"Yes, then we can always keep baby Shalia smelling sweet." There's a slight coo to his voice when he speaks that makes me want to snicker. He sounds so much like his dad and grandfather in that voice they reserve for infants.

Not that Shalia has much hair to wash. My baby got her lighter locks from her father. Right now, they're wispy and baby fine.

"When she's old enough to play with me, I'm gonna take good care of her. The best ever."

"I know you will, sweetie. I have no doubts. Do you want to hold her? Sit on the sofa right here and I'll set her in your arms."

He scrambles to where I point, where his little arm can rest on the edge and help him hold her up. She's still tiny, but she's dead weight for a five-year old's care.

"How's school going?" I ask him as I settle Shalia in his arms.

I know from experience, he'll keep up the conversation but will never pull his gaze from her.

"So far, I like it. Mostly because mom's teaching us and we's gonna get a break when the baby comes. That means I can help you with sweet Shally and then go home and help my mommy."

"Do you suppose you'll have a brother or a sister?"

He shrugs his little shoulders. "Dunno. Grumpa Brachard wants a girl and my other Grampy wants a boy, so I'll have someone to play with."

"What do you want?"

"A sister, I guess. So Shally will have a best friend, just like you and momma are best friends. But Auntie Vin says you were her best friend first."

I snicker. I can already tell Shally's going to be a nickname for my little one.

"Vin is still my best friend too. And if you have a sister, then you'll take care of two little girls."

"Yes." The air around him thickens and... sweetens. I catch the scent of something like honey, if honey had a smell instead of taste. "But it's okay because one day Shally's going to grow up and be my *anyasa*. *Gi anyasa*," he corrects. "And we're gunna have two little girls too, but they're going to be born at the same time, not like it is with Shally and my new sister. Shally's gunna be a little older but not much."

An eerie feeling washes over me... one I haven't felt since I did with Hannah, five years earlier when Brun died during a sparring practice. Since then, Brachard has decided to change the ruling that proclaimed scarring a royal is an instant death sentence.

Just then, Hannah's voice calls out at my cabin door. "Yoohoo! *Hyi-ak!*"

"Come in."

She enters, then sucks in a huge whiff of air, which expands her already full belly. She's going into labor very soon.

Her eyes grow wide. "Is that what I think I smell? The other realm?" Her eyes drift over my goose-fleshed arm. "Bakog, did you make a prediction?"

"Oh, yah," he agrees easily. "I guess so. I seen it in my mind."

"Shalia will be his mate," I say softly. "And they're going to have two little girls, born at the same time. Not like Shalia and his sister, who will be best friends but born at different times. Right, Baki?"

"Yep," he says happily, still peering down at Shalia. She licks her lips with a tiny tongue, making him laugh, and then she smiles at his laughter.

"And we'll be grandmas," Hannah says, looping her arm through mine.

I can't help but smile. "Your son inherited your gift."

"He did," she agrees, rubbing her belly. "I came to get you all. Everyone is gathering for dinner."

"Aww, mommy. I just got comfortable with Shally!" Bakog tries to fiercely scowl but looks kind of comical instead. Little tyke is missing the hairy eyebrows.

"How about if I let you hold her after you're done with your dinner?" I ask.

"Okay," he says happily, sure that he's bargained for more time. "You hear that, Shally? I'm gonna eat so I can grow big and strong and protect you."

Hannah places her arm over her heart and mouths to me, "So cute."

I nod, picking up the satchel with diapers and a change of clothes. Then I take Shalia from Bakog's arms and, wanting to help, he swings my satchel over one shoulder, which practically dwarfs him. Hannah holds out her hand for him to take and the four of us make our way down to the main building. Up ahead, I see the horses in the corral and I'm sure Latsil is washing up or has already entered the main hall looking for me.

Sure enough, we're eating outside today, the huge double doors open because males are bringing the tables and benches out. Bakog whoops when Brun tosses him up into the air, and Latsil bends down to kiss me, then kisses Shalia's head.

"How are you, beautiful?"

"Happy now that my handsome mate is home."

He closes his eyes and sighs deeply. "I never get tired of hearing that."

I stand on tiptoe to kiss his lips. "I never get tired of saying it."

"I finished eating early!" Brachard bellows as he walks toward us with his fingers wiggling. "I can take the wee one and my grandson to sit under a tree. Come, my boy. Someone bring Bakog a plate!"

He doesn't wait for an answer as he grabs Shalia from my arms and then kisses the top of her head. "Are you growing hair? Why, I think you are, yes, I do," he coos in a high-pitched tone as he nuzzles her.

"Smell it," Bakog says excitedly. "Doesn't she smell like the sweetest brat ever?"

"Come, my love," I say to Latsil. "Let's join Brun and Hannah, hmm?"

Bessica makes room for us on the bench, her three-year-old hugging her knees. Despite drinking her teas, she was the first whore after Bakog's birth to get pregnant.

As soon as her little girl, Daisy, sees "Grumpy Brachard" with Bakog and Shalia, she runs on chubby little legs over there. Brachard's face lights up as he greets the toddler.

"Did you hear? Grunalda, out of all of us, has finally allowed Gorvan to come inside her," Bessica says.

I can't help but snicker at the way she phrases it.

"Whaat?" Hannah screeches. "She wants to have her own whelp now?"

"She says Daisy, Bakog, and Shalia are cute enough, so she'll go ahead and try."

"My ass," Vinshesa says. "Bet you Gorvan offered her a bribe."

I laugh the hardest because yesterday Grun offered me quite a bit of coin to purchase expensive silk fabrics in an array of colors the next time I shop. She wants sundresses like me and Hannah wear. So yes, I believe she accepted Gorvan's bribe.

"That male is so whipped over her it's disgusting," Vin says. "I'll be the last holdout."

"Don't make it too long," I say. "You know Hannah ends up getting pregnant each time one of us does."

"True!" Hannah grins. "Don't make me end up with sixteen brats."

"I'd be good with twelve," Brun says, nuzzling his mate.

"Here, beautiful," Kreele says, offering Vinshesa a lavender lemonade from the kitchens. I haven't seen her touch ale for so long, it's hard to remember how bleary-eyed she used to look.

"Look at our 'hard-assed' king," Bessica says. "Aga. Can you remind him of the way he used to bellow? That high-pitched squeal your male has now makes me grind my teeth."

"Makes me want to braid his hair," Vin says.

"Well, if you whores would stop popping out brats, he wouldn't have to talk like that. It's really your own fault," Aga says.

"Huh. It's her son and daughter-in-law who started it," Vin mouths.

"Oh, shush, you. I'd hate for Brachard to get the idea in his head that Kreele needs a son." Aga's threat is mild, but Vinshesa shuts up.

Kreele whispers in her ear and by the way her cheeks turn a darker green, I'm pretty sure it's naughty.

I lean back onto Latsil's chest, and the familiar feeling of warmth and protection fills me. I inhale deeply, getting his familiar and cherished scent into my lungs.

"You and my beautiful daughter have changed my life forever," he rumbles.

"Aye, just as you've changed mine, my perfect mate."

"Sometimes I think this is a dream. I can't believe life is this good."

"We both had horrible first relationships. Now we deserve to have the happy one. We get to watch our beautiful daughter grow up and mate the love of her life."

"An orc loves forever, you know."

"I've heard that somewhere," I tease. "And it's a good thing. I'm keeping you until the end of time, my love."

When his lips fall to mine, all the other sounds of our large, loveable, and somewhat obnoxious family fade away.

Thank you for reading! Bought By The Orc[1] is available now!

I hope everyone enjoyed book two, Saved By The Orc! When I wrote Owned By The Orc for the Monster Brides series (an arranged-marriage collaboration with seven other authors), I couldn't stop Joanna and Latsil from speaking to me, yet I didn't have time to stop writing Hannah and Brun's story before the series deadline. In this story, the only unmated orc in Brun's royal guard left is Azorr, so he may get his book to make this series a trilogy, but it won't be until the end of summer. I need to wrap up the last book in The Match Program, tentatively titled The Monster's Mate.

Also, my Xeno Sapiens (The Genetically Altered Humans nineteen-book series) is leaving KU. They'll still be available with Amazon, but because KU is exclusive, they can't be on any other sites. So, by the end of summer, they'll be available at all retailers everywhere. Yay!

If you have a moment, I'd appreciate if you'd leave a review for Saved By The Orc. It doesn't have to be long, and it doesn't have to be fancy! Anything will do. Reviews encourage authors to keep writing wonderful stories that carry you away from real life for a while.

Feel free to follow on Facebook, TikTok, or Instagram, or even Bookbub, and sign up for my newsletter on my website to get news about upcoming book release dates and free bonus material exclusive for you. No spamming, ever. Just an effort to keep you in the loop. And please read on to see if you'd be interested in any of my other books. Thank you again!

Sign up for my newsletter to get more up-to-date news. It's usually sent once or twice a month: https://renamarks.com/newsletter/

---

1.   https://books2read.com/u/3nBxD5

Owned By The Orc[1]

Monster Brides Series
Rena Marks

I REFUSED MARRIAGE, so one was arranged for me, but he's not human. He's orc.

Hannah of the humans: Marriage between an orc and a human is forbidden unless your village needs the protection of their clan, in which case they're willing to sacrifice any maiden who refuses to do their bidding.

Since my father is the lord overseer, I have no choice. I'm to be an orc's arranged bride.

I am Lady Hannah Montierge, despite my title being stripped along with my dignity.

Brun, son of Brachard: One human wormed her way into my heart as children. But she disappeared without a word. When I'm told I must marry a human, I never expected it would be her.

But Hannah pretends she doesn't know me, claiming an illness as a child stole her memories. She wants to believe I'm a savage beast and

---

1. https://www.amazon.com/Owned-Monster-Brides-Rena-Marks-ebook/dp/B0BW3621MD

not the childhood friend who spent hours promising her we'd be together forever.

I'm about to keep that promise. It's her choice as to which.

Other books in the series:

Saved By The Orc

<u>Bought By The Orc</u>[2]

Adored By The Orc

Zearn[1]

A Sci-fi Holiday Tail
Stranded With An Alien Series
Rena Marks

A MYSTERIOUS ALIEN planet celebrates their own version of merry holidays. Their wonderful gift-giving idea? Earth ladies as stocking stuffers.

Alyssa: As one of the few female Earthians who works in space, I'm not about to give up my career for marriage and babies. I scorn the idiots who created the podcast "Earth Girls Are Horny." Unfortunately, they've gone viral in a whole new way, calling unwanted attention from galaxies far, far away. The planet Thropian is one secretive and unknown planet who are paying big money to have a bride shipped in a pod to drop down in time for their holiday games. And our horny Earth girls? The volunteers are a mile long, even when it's unknown what the mysterious Thropians look like.

Just not me. No, my job is to test the pod before the actual prize is sent. I'll earn a boatload of money for *not* being a bride.

---

1. https://www.amazon.com/Zearn-Sci-fi-Holiday-Rena-Marks-ebook/dp/B0BHKRFWZ3/ref=sr_1_2?keywords=zearn+rena+marks&qid=1671310077&sr=8-2

Zearn: A mate is the last thing on my mind, especially one from a dismal planet who offer themselves to complete strangers as prizes. The utter arrogance is astounding. But when a female lands in the danger zone of our competitive Twelve Days of Cheneca, I'm dispatched as the lead hunter to track her down, and to keep her safe. I do not expect a female who is as much a warrior as me.

A female who is worthy of me. A prize who marries me in the traditional way during the celebrations of our holidays.

With her mouth.

* This book is part of the Stranded With an Alien shared world.

Matched To The Monster[1]

The Match Program Series

I'M HUMAN. HE'S NOT.

Lilaina: As the First Daughter of Planet Earth, it's my duty to set an example. When we enter an agreement to re-build the planet, our prized offerings for bargaining are our young, eligible females, starting with me. It's my place to lead by example and I'm only too eager. I can hardly wait to see what handsome, mysterious stranger has been matched for me. Who will sweep me off my feet?

I never expected tentacles.

Juris: The Match Program put together by the Britonian race assures my people that mates from a human planet would be a perfect pair up for us in exchange for our plentiful gold. But those females think of us as monsters. Instead of them allowing us to honor them, they shiver in fear and wish for us to treat them as slaves. They have been taught this way from birth.

On a planet of beautiful, plentiful females repressed by their own males, who are really the monsters?

This is the first book in the Matched Program Series.

The gorgeous species called Britonians had left their planet with a dying sun. They reached an agreement with Earth to clean up our ruined planet with their modern technology in exchange for a new place to live. If it were up to women, we'd allow them to live just to look at them. The Brits are amazing, gold skin, tall and muscular, like avenging angels.

---

1. https://www.amazon.com/Matched-Monster-Romance-Steamy-Program-ebook/dp/B09KQD2TY4

When they hear that most of our men died in the third World War, leaving the sexes vastly mismatched, they offer to begin a Match Program with a distant planet in need of females. It will be completely professional, personality-matching, compatibility, and the possibility of procreation. Plus, the human females will have a guaranteed choice after six months: Remain with your alien mate or come home to Earth.

None of us expected the gorgeous alien species to introduce us to horrifying monsters.

Book 1—Matched To The Monster (Juris & Lilaina)[2]
Book 2—Matched To the Monster Too (Stratek & Tessa)[3]
Also available in a book set!
Book 3—Wanted By The Monster (Jaire & Anya)[4]
Book 4—Wanting The Monster (Relion & Tera)[5]
Also available in a book set!
Book 5—My Monster, My Choice (Elex & Christina)
Book 6—My Matched Monster (Tiran & River)
Book 7—The Monster's Bride (Bronan & Isabel)
Book 8—The Monster's Mate (Skiden & Lucy)

2.	https://www.amazon.com/Matched-Monster-Romance-Steamy-Program-ebook/dp/B09KQD2TY4

3.	https://www.amazon.com/gp/product/B09RQ52WRX?notRedirectToS-DP=1&ref_=dbs_mng_calw_1&storeType=ebooks

4.	https://www.amazon.com/gp/product/B0B2F1S9YQ?notRedirectToS-DP=1&ref_=dbs_mng_calw_2&storeType=ebooks

5.	https://www.amazon.com/gp/product/B0B6HHS9Z4?notRedirectToS-DP=1&ref_=dbs_mng_calw_3&storeType=ebooks

Maddie Mine[1]

Boulder Bear Shifters

S he's on the run from a monster. But I'm here to protect her. No one ever expected me to fail.

Maddie had a plan to run away from her ex-husband. She never expected to leave late and have to stay at a small mountain lodge last minute. She didn't expect the owner to be sexy and grumpy—or to shift into a bear right before her eyes. Now that she did see it, though, he isn't going to let her go. But this time, being held captive has a completely different meaning. He's caring and protective and she doesn't want to run. This time, she's found a family.

Until the life she ran from threatens to invade. Can the bears protect her? Or will she pay the price for daring to leave?

Boulder Bear Shifters – Maddie Mine[2]

---

1. https://www.amazon.com/Maddie-Mine-Boulder-Bear-Shifters-ebook/dp/B0BKH39W6W/ref=sr_1_1?crid=3A3WZJHDXW3HB&keywords=maddie+mine+rena+marks&qid=1667082906&s=digital-text&sprefix=maddie+mine+rena+mark%2Cdigital-text%2C452&sr=1-1

2.   https://www.amazon.com/Maddie-Mine-Boulder-Bear-Shifters-ebook/dp/B0BKH39W6W/ref=sr_1_1?crid=3A3WZJHDXW3HB&keywords=maddie+mine+re-

My Alien Baby[1]

Book 1 of the Lost & Found Series
Rena Marks, A. Blake

♪♪**IVORY BELLOWS FELL down a well. Ivory Bellows woke up in hell. Better listen to the big blue giant, zip your lip, and hush. Better not stare at his son who makes you blush.** ♪♪

Imagine if you were a giant, fifteen-foot alien from another planet and found a strange being unconscious in a foreign object. . .a flying pod. The creature is tiny enough to be a child and you'd have such a big heart, you'd want to adopt this poor orphaned child, right?

Only. . .what if the full-grown human you found didn't know she was your child? What if she thought she was your dinner instead?

The Raza are a people full of honor, faith, and family. Especially Havak of the Jaha clan. His first yun is of his heart, not his blood. But when his mate dies and his beloved yun goes off into the world to study other people and languages, the Creators give him a second chance at life. He happens upon a strange little yun of a species unlike anything he's ever seen.

A strange, five-fingered species.

When the yun wakes and screams, he gives her a bub-bub, wraps her in a pu-pu, and packs her in his sket to bring home.

His huge heart is filled with love for his second adopted yun.

Ivory Bellows wakes up in a strange land filled with blue giants. They threaten her in their strange language, shove a plug in her mouth to keep her quiet and take her home to fatten her up. And marinate her.

---

1. https://www.amazon.com/My-Alien-Baby-Found-Romance-ebook/dp/B08YWNBRDW?ref_=ast_sto_dp

They must marinate her when she sleeps, because she's swollen and always needs to pee.

Oh, God. She's dinner. It's only a matter of time until they decide when.

But when a hot new alien arrives, the only way she can keep sane is to pretend he's her husband and she's his wife and everything is hunky-dory fine.

Thank God this new arrival, Iik, doesn't know her language.

Yet.

Space Babies[1]

Book 1 of the Purple People Series
Rena Marks

AN ANTIQUATED SHIP, rotating through the galaxy of a deserted planet, bears immediate investigation.

Helian Six boards the abandoned vessel to find the long-lost inhabitants in a state of stasis. But the systems are failing, and half a dozen have woken up. The planet below shows long dead bodies, poisoned by the scum of space, a species known as Gorgians.

Strangely, the few who have awakened are much smaller than their planetary predecessors. And not very intelligent. Determined to believe the cute, tiny beings are not pets, the crew of Helian Six decide to train the small warriors to defend the planet. They become the laughingstock of patrol, however, after they commit and realize it will take twenty-two cycles to "rear" the inhabitants.

So they do what any intelligent males would do. Kidnap teachers. And if the females can't manage to avert their eyes from their buff physiques, well, score!

Book 1—Space Babies
Book 2—Baby Soldiers In Space
Book 3—Baby Butterfly Kisses
Book 4—Titi
Book 5—Rock-A-Bye Babies In Space

---

1. https://www.amazon.com/Space-Babies-Purple-People-Book-ebook/dp/B073V428YP

Xeno Sapiens[1]

CATCH UP WITH THE FIRST novel in the series! The original Xeno Sapiens story.

Futuristic earth finds alien DNA and creates a new species of hybrids in hidden labs. It's up to two small females to teach these beings they're worthy, and beautiful, and loved . . . and to save them from mankind.

My name is Dr. Robyn Saraven. Earth has changed greatly in recent years, the governments of the world merging into one united front, the Global Government. Disease, starvation, and prejudice have been eradicated from our existence, and it appears our growth as spiritual beings is finally on track.

But the discovery of alien DNA pairs a prestigious research facility with our government to create new beings. Suddenly our spiritual growth is halted when mankind plays God. Like old Earth, our modern-day world has to deal with prejudice, corruption, and greed.

Or was it always there, lurking beneath the surface?

Book 1—Xeno Sapiens

Book 2—Earth-Ground

Book 3—Siren

---

1. https://www.amazon.com/Xeno-Sapiens-Genetically-Altered-Humans-ebook/dp/B07BGTSMC4/ref=sr_1_1?crid=3GMGFLCLL3TXO&keywords=xeno+sapiens+rena+marks&qid=1667053943&s=digital-text&sprefix=xeno+sapiens+rena+marks%2Cdigital-text%2C278&sr=1-1

Book 4—Beast's Beauty
Book 5—Almost Human
Book 6—Forbidden Touches
Book 7—Coveting Ava
Book 8—For Everly
Book 9—Assassin's Mate
Book 10—Sextet
Book 11—Tempting Tempest
Book 12—Falling For Trance
Book 13—Damaged Goods
Book 14—Alien's Bride
Book 15—Dual Lives
Book 16—Reson's Lesson
Book 17—A Mate For Max
Book 18—Dragon's Mate
Book 19—Fated

Alien Stolen

Rena Marks

OUR WORLD IS DIFFERENT from anything we've ever known. Years ago, aliens came to live among us. They claim to be the good guys, and yet every day, humans go missing—never to be heard from again.

Sian and her family resist the leadership of the new regime, along with dozens of other factions across the world. However, without electricity, they're at a loss as to how to communicate with each other to band together for strength in numbers. For that reason, they fight alone. When her father and best friend are captured by the military, she pretends to be a pleasure worker to infiltrate the base. Unbeknownst to her, a pleasure worker *has* been summoned to service a new breed of alien—one with a known weakness. Sex drains his strength.

None of the militia realizes that when a Nisibian comes across his mate, he doesn't lose his power . . . but instead transfers it to her.

Drunk on the power of being a female Rambo, Sian decides to steal the massive alien for herself. This much power at her fingertips could tip the scales in the resistance fight for humans.

Abducted

BOOK 1 IN THE BLUE Barbarian series.

Alien abductions are real.

I was the third female awakened aboard the spacecraft that specialized in kidnapping females. Their mission? To sell us to other galaxies.

Human female Numbers One and Two didn't make it, but I was lucky. I was able to comprehend the instruction from Drakar, a caged abductee from the planet Blaedonia. I live only because of his warning to me not to fight the aliens who have me on the table. Together, we formulate a plan for escape for both us and the ten other unawakened Earthlings.

Lucky for Drakar, the spaceship crash-lands back on his planet. Unlucky for the Earthlings, we'll never be able to travel back home.

We'll have to learn to adapt.

Book 1—Abducted

Book 2—Stranded

Book 3—Taken

Book 4—Captive

Book 5—Stolen

Book 6—Betrayed

Artificial Intelligence

Rena Marks

THE SIRIAN GALAXY HAS blown itself up during a war that mimicked that of the destruction of her own planet, Terra. No stranger to slavery, Arian has escaped from the planet Zeta where she's been raised to breed royalty.

The Artificial Intelligence is a collective unit from the Sirian Planet B. They'd warned the leaders that a civil war would destroy the galaxy to no avail. In order to escape being destroyed along with the rest, they inserted their intelligence into the computer system.

Imagine Arian's surprise when she encounters a huge piece of chipped planet, which her computer claims to have ancient Sirian artifacts buried in its hollowed core.

Nothing can possibly be alive. The contamination gases from the nuclear war have destroyed everything in sight. But Arian is a scavenger, and these are ancient artifacts . . .

Unfortunately, her hacked computer never tells her the artifacts are actually metal skeletons whose bodies need to be grown into dangerously hot men.

Stargazer Series

IN 1692, A STARSHIP carrying volunteers arrived on planet Earth near a small town called Salem, Massachusetts. The long journey across many light years caused the female inhabitants aboard drastic memory loss. It was already known when they would arrive on Earth, they would have no memories of who and what they really were. They would be as helpless as newborn lambs.

The goal was to breed with Earthlings, to prevent their own race from dying out. If it was successful, years later more Stargazers would be sent to co-exist with the humans on Planet Earth.

But alas—the females were slaughtered.

Book 1—**The Hunter**
Dante and Kele
Book 2 —**The Enforcer**
Diamond and Felicia
Book 3 —**The Defender**
Hayze and Cassio
Book 4 —**The Protector**
Neo and Jessie
Book 5 —**The Guardian**
Vesta and Bay
Book 6 —**The Destroyer**
Jace and Mia

Also by Rena Marks

GENETICALLY ALTERED Humans Series: Xeno Sapiens, Earth-Ground, Siren, Beast's Beauty, Almost Human, Forbidden Touches, Coveting Ava, For Everly, Assassin's Mate, Sextet, Tempting Tempest, Falling For Trance, Damaged Goods, Alien's Bride, Dual Lives, Reson's Lesson, A Mate For Max, Dragon's Mate, Fated

My Alien Baby

The Matched Program: Matched to the Monster, Matched to the Monster, Too!, Wanted by the Monster

Alien Stolen

Born Again

Magic Gems

Wanton Sins Series: Demonic Passions, Demonic Pleasures, Demonic Power

Shared By Wolves

Enticing Fate

SuperNatural Sharing Series: Forgotten Kisses, Remembered Kisses, Whispered Kisses

Kiss Me Before I Die

Stargazer Series: The Hunter, The Enforcer, The Defender, The Protector, The Guardian, The Destroyer

Blue Barbarian Series: Abducted, Stranded, Taken, Captive, Stolen, Betrayed

The AI Series: Artificial Intelligence, Serepto's Story

Purple People Series: Space Babies, Baby Soldiers In Space, Baby Butterfly Kisses, Titi, Baby Butterfly Kisses

Chasing Violet—written with C.L. Scholey

Made in the USA
Middletown, DE
05 July 2025

10131807R10102